Science Fiktion

THE
SEAGULL
LIBRARY OF
GERMAN
LITERATURE

Franz Fühmann

Science Fiktion

Translated by

Andrew B.B. Hamilton and Claire van den Broek

LONDON NEW YORK CALCUTTA

This publication has been supported by a grant
from the Goethe-Intitut India

Seagull Books, 2022

Originally published in German as Franz Fühmann: *Saiäns-Fiktschen*

First published in English translation by Seagull Books, 2018

ISBN 978 1 8030 9 184 6

British Library Cataloguing-in-Publication Data
A catalogue record for this book is available from the British Library

Typeset by Seagull Books, Calcutta, India
Printed and bound by WordsWorth India, New Delhi, India

Contents

Preface

When a young reader first asked me if I write—his German pronunciation of the English words sounded like something altogether different—*saiäns-fiktschen*, I responded immediately: No! I thought of the science fiction genre: the little I had read I did not like, and I was not inclined to add to the world's supply of it. Later on, I read more, and here and there I found something to my liking, as for instance the idea that a starfish, informed by its radial structure, does not conceive of binary decisions, but rather thinks of everything along a close continuum.

But still, I didn't want to write science fiction.

Then, during a bad crisis, I think it was in 1974, I wrote the first story in this book, "Helplessness." I wrote it in the attempt to overcome an existential crisis, and in its unreal world I hit upon a form that allowed me to put into words what was troubling me so much.

I had to accept that words had become agonizing. The journal *Sinn und Form* published the story, and it was not long before I heard from a reader that I had badly missed the point of the genre of science fiction: I had packed in all these physics problems in a way that was too trashy for serious science fiction, and too serious for simple pulp fiction. Aha. Being entirely unqualified to discuss the nature of science fiction, I limited myself to pointing out in reply that it had not been my intention to write science fiction. My reader wouldn't have it. Genre is genre, he wrote back, and as a Marxist I must know that it doesn't matter what I intend, subjectively, but rather what I in fact do, objectively. Good. A misunderstanding. To avoid repeating it, from now on I will declare such stories to be not science fiction, but *saiäns-fiktschen*.

For I had noticed that the cast of characters, Janno, Jirro, and Pavlo, created the opportunity, on account of their somewhat abstract character, to bring to light other difficulties, in order to better address them. The sort of difficulties that are so hard to portray, because even though they are based in reality, they expand well beyond the bounds of what is realistic. Such hypertrophied feeling is in the domain of emotions the equivalent of what is known in the rational domain as thinking something through all the way to its conclusion, except that rational thinking as such has a different kind of rigor and objectivity than fear, or terror, or guessing, or affliction. "To fear something to its conclusion" ends in catastrophe; "guessing something to its conclusion" rules out any alternatives; "thinking someone to his conclusion" means to annihilate him; "to be terrified at something to its conclusion" doesn't just seem ghastly—it makes the ghastly omnipresent, ubiquitous, and absolute. The world of these stories is an unreal end times, the sum and consequence of all that is negative in humanity's expressions of its own development. But all these endings have their beginnings, and we should work to guard against these, especially where everything begins: in the personal sphere.

Alas, misunderstandings cannot be avoided, and in order to neutralize at least one, let me say: *saiänsfiktschen* does not propose a utopian system, at least not a complete one, and makes no claims at prophecy. When no one knows what will happen tomorrow, how could one possibly know what the year 3456 will bring? There is hardly any trace of science: loose references to a social space, details that differ from case to case in each story, with inconsistent and often contradictory terminology—don't look for any completeness here. The stories appear in the order in which they were written. Twice while writing I confused two characters. This happens in life, too: suddenly someone entirely different than you thought is standing there. So why not in literature too?

Science Fiktion, then. A hybrid. Not to be taken seriously as science fiction, but as *saiäns-fiktschen* just as serious as the written form of the spoken word: something one step removed. It shows results, not processes, however process-like these results are. They are, these stories, completely terminal points, in the realm of heaped contradictions, where stagnation is the only driving force. Development as the impossibility of development. The sleep of reason, says Goya, gives birth to monstrosities; the heaping of contradictions brings forth monsters. I will hardly be able to defend myself if someone calls these stories monsters.

In response to the question I am sure is coming—whether I will write any more *saiäns-fiktschen*—I answer immediately: No!

Helplessness

"It is quite simple," said Janno. "Every attempt to bend space failed; so now we are bending time. Don't think of it visually—the word "bending" is just a figure of speech. It's a bending into the fifth dimension. When time, or to be more precise, the space-time continuum, bends into the fifth dimension, a piece of the future overlaps with the present, and time forms a loop, which crosses the present moment twice. It's really quite a simple principle."

"Then why haven't I heard of this before?"

Janno shrugged his shoulders politely, apologetically. "The procedure is meaningless in practical terms: the radius of the loop is miniscule, usually fractions of a microsecond—what practical use for that is there?"

"Can you even measure such a small increment of time?"

"Only on a subatomic scale, but Pavlo takes advantage of the fact that the loop expands into a causality knot, up to a few seconds or even a minute."

"But that must be tremendously signif—"

"No, it's still irrelevant. The effect is localized and is based on the person doing the experiment; it has no military application, and the personal element is considered insignificant. Society doesn't really care if someone finds out a little bit sooner or later what is going to happen to him anyway."

"That means you only see your own future?"

"Just you and your immediate vicinity. That's why Pavlo got in trouble: individualistic fooling around, prognostic formalism, elitist intellectualism—you know all about it. So now he only does it occasionally, in private, for the friends of his friends, but only for a little something, you understand."

The visitor nodded automatically, as though that much went without saying. "And that causality effect, the knot you were talking about, when does it happen?"

"A chemo-computer calculates that for you; the formulas are complicated, certain tensor additions, which are very sensitive to certain constants, what they call AC-Quotients, and then the size of the cycloids—but don't worry about that." He looked plaintively at his visitor. "Does this mean you really won't just forget about the whole thing? I strongly advise against it."

"Is it painful?" asked the visitor, a smartly-dressed man in his mid-forties. His voice betrayed the layman's fear of new gadgets. Janno laughed, but with no trace of happiness. "Physically, of course not . . . "

"But?"

"Morally. That's why I'm warning you. There's a feeling of helplessness that gets everyone, no matter how hard you try to fight it. Especially if you do it more than once, but Pavlo refuses to do that anymore, and most people don't want to anyway. The procedure itself is quite primitive. You dunk your eyes into a tank filled with a kind of plasma—no, don't worry, it's not a fire, not electricity, just a strange, pale blue flickering light. As a matter of fact, you don't feel anything, no heat, no smell, and no aftereffects. As soon as this flicker, a decomposing logo-alkaloid, works its way into the pores of your aura, the chemo-computer can calculate the necessary coefficients, and then you see the overlapping interval of time from your future. The computer calculates its distance from the current point in time. You have to keep your eyes open, but you don't feel a thing—except of course in your wallet. Pavlo's raised his price: you'll have to pay a pound. But really, I wi—"

The visitor interrupted to say that he had imagined there was more to it. Even when Janno pointed out that a pound was enough to buy a liter of the good stuff, or six food credits, with fruit and ground coffee, and that even for a citizen of the third income class, such money was no chickenfeed, he replied that this was true, but at the same time, he would surely never have such a fine opportunity . . .

Janno waved his hands in irritation. "Once in a lifetime, that's what they all say, and it's true, but not the way you think. I'm trying to save you from having to pay for something that's just going to eat away at you. You could save yourself all this trouble simply by realizing that you can always see the future, as soon as it stops being the future. Think of what the present was one minute ago. Every *now* used to be a *later*; every *is* was once a *will be*. The way you are pressing your lips right now, for example, used to belong completely to the future. Now just imagine a blue flickering light, and yourself inside it, as you raise the corners of your mouth just so—there, that's the show you are so eager for. You won't see much more than that, and you could have saved yourself the feeling of helplessness—and a full pound. You can paint the picture of such minutiae yourself: blue flickering light, and looking yourself in the eye like in a mirror. It really is trivial."

The visitor replied enthusiastically. "But only because daily life is trivial, or rather: the character of time—I don't mean of this particular time, though also that, but time as such, as a category. Its essence is that it passes, and it would be foolish to spend money to prove that what is happening now was not there before when it was the future—but always an unverifiable future! *That* is trivial! But it is possible to actually test a prediction about the future; that is more than sensational, even if it doesn't please your superiors. I think you have no idea what you have here! Obviously you are jaded from having seen it a hundred times, but for someone coming here for the first time . . . "

Janno wanted to interject something, but his visitor cut him off. "I beg you, lay it out for me systematically; you aren't going to change my mind. So I dunk my head into the flickering light and open my eyes—what do I see? The future *and* the present?"

"You see the future loop, but the rest of your senses stay with us in the present. For example, you hear our voices, but you see what's coming."

"And you see what I see?"

"We can see both the present and the future, but the future only as an electrical image in your brain, so rather imprecisely. But we do recognize contours, even physiognomies, but most of all motion, so whether you are standing still or walking. Or to be more precise: whether you see yourself standing still or walking."

"And how does time pass? Forwards or backwards?"

"If we could bend space it would run backwards, but only from the present into the past. It runs forward through the time loop, and you see a segment of the future, but only the overlapping section. Say you see one minute into the future. That doesn't mean you see the full sixty seconds, at most you would see the last five, that is—if you begin looking at time zero—the seconds fifty-six through sixty, while seconds one through five continue to flow normally. We outside see the present and the future, the future only dimly, while you see it quite vividly, but only see it. Fifty-five, no, fifty-one seconds later—"

"—come the five seconds that I just saw in the blue light."

"Of course. The very ones. In the fifty-sixth second, the fifty-sixth second happens; in the fifty-seventh, the fifty-seventh, and so on until the sixtieth second, and then time proceeds into the part you didn't see. The loop has rewound; the overlapping portion has run out; the future keeps turning into the present, and time—except for the micro-phenomena—keeps going only in one dimension. Only . . . "

"Don't bother. You're not going to talk me out of it."

"I just wanted you to know that you don't see a whole minute, at most the length of a few seconds."

The visitor's eyes lit up, and Janno's eyes blazed back in response.

"But what if," said the visitor, deep in thought, wondering whether he had found an objection that would trouble Janno, "what if I do something completely different from what I saw in the light?"

Janno looked at him with exasperation. "See, it's that kind of hubris that makes you feel so helpless afterward. And then you'll start making lame excuses! Once you've seen that for you, too, it happens just like you saw it. It's always the same reaction. You start off with brash confidence: 'It won't happen to me!' Then, after you try it, you sing a different tune. Finally you start questioning reality. No one wants to know that it's always the same, that he behaves just like everyone else. It is a double helplessness: in the face of the immutability of fate, and at how unexceptional you are. At first everyone thinks that their *wanting* it will do the trick: 'I see what I am supposed to be about to do, so I must be able to change it. It is a matter of will!' And what's more, he believes in *his* own free will: all of the others may get duped—but he'll show this so-called fate how it works! And then to have his helplessness shown to him, and, as I said, with doubled force: first his *helplessness*, and then his *particular* helplessness; the power of fate, and his own interchangeability with everyone else! Everyone acts the same way at the beginning: the same questions, the same hope, the same arguments, the same illusions, and then the same defensive excuses when the same thing happens to him that happens to everyone else. Except of course for the cases where the loop is so small that you only see yourself a moment in advance, that is, still sitting there looking into the blue light. But even then the helplessness is inevitable; you can feel its terrible rush, and even if you only saw five seconds, it knocks you out. And then the pitiful self-deception! The loop's radius must be too small, that future must have been the past; someone has played a mean trick on me, or whatever other excuses they come up with. But that's all only symptoms. It feels like choking when you recognize your own helplessness."

The visitor looked ready for a fight.

"You see!" Janno said. "They all look at me like that. That's the future for you! I knew exactly what you were going to do."

He opened the desk drawer.

"With no way to check," said the visitor. "With no way to check, anyone could say that! And," he continued confidently, "and as for the experiment, you are forgetting that I have a degree in logic. And my syllogism is irrefutable. What I will do is my own free decision, and I can change my decision, which means that everything that I will do in the future is subject to change. A syllogism of the Bamalip form, a form that dates back to the time of the great Galenus. Who could argue against him? And who could keep me from changing my own future action? Answer me that!"

While the visitor was speaking, Janno had taken a plaque out of the desk drawer and held it up for the visitor to read:

Your question will boil down to the following:

Who could stop me from doing the opposite of what I see, since I am after all free in my own decision?

"How nice," admitted the visitor. "You saw my question coming, but of course I was going to ask it. I'd still like to know the answer."

"The experiment will give you the answer, but then your problem will be how to explain it. I have my own theory, involving AC-attraction, but we can talk about that later. Then you'll also see that your premises are false, even though your syllogism is sound. And now let's go, before Pavlo gets too whalified."

"Whalified?"

"Never mind. I mean drowning in the juice. It's terrible how he can get."

"Let's go over it again," said the visitor, as they were going down the tunnel of the blue corridor. "I dunk my eyes into blue light and I see a little piece of the near future, let's say one minute away. This means that I can see in advance what I'm going to do later. Is that right so far?"

"Right," Janno confirmed, turning into green corridor. "Right, but you only see the final few seconds."

"But the final seconds of what is going to happen, and I see my own actions—is that right? Excellent. Now I am facing an either-or: I will either sit motionlessly at the table, or I will not, that is, I will walk around, or point to someone, or talk, or something. Sit motionless or something else—however I act, it will have to be one of these two, right?"

"You are doing your logic degree proud," Janno said drily. "Move or don't move, one or the other."

"Very good. And you outside can see what I see?"

"The picture quality is good enough for that. We could also film what you see."

"All the better; that makes it objective. Now let's assume you and I—and the camera—all see me sitting still at the table. Then, at time X, I will simply start walking around the room."

"No, you won't!"

"And why not?"

"Because that's not what you saw! If you see yourself sitting there in the blue light, then when time X comes around, you'll be sitting exactly where you saw."

"And if I just don't stay seated?"

"Then you wouldn't have seen yourself sitting."

"But I see myself sitting and then get up anyway!"

"But you can't, because you won't have seen that."

The visitor sighed. When Janno said, "Trust me, that's how it will happen." he almost lost his composure: "Your cleverness is really disheartening! I know that you have a degree in causality, but you must have gone wrong somewhere. Your experiment must be a self-deception."

"Type number six," said Janno casually.

They strolled through the doors of the yellow corridor.

"Run through it with me," begged the visitor. "Please. Think about my example again. We saw me sitting at the table. That would be, let's say, second fifty-six in the future but second one in the present."

"You formulate it wonderfully."

"So, between second one and second fifty-six, a portion of real time passes?"

"Indeed. Fifty-one seconds of it."

"And I can do what I like during this time?"

"Using what you call your free will."

"I will use it, you can be sure of that! Now I see what's going on. This whole production is supposed to sap my decisive energy. Your warnings weaken the will to resistance, and the subject falls into a self-hypnosis, which convinces him to be dependent on what he sees. But not me. I won't fall for it! I will say aloud what I saw, and then I will do just the opposite. In the first case I would walk around the room; or else, if I had seen myself walking, I would stay seated and sit there quietly."

"No, you will do what you saw."

The visitor looked at him mistrustfully. "Say, do you really want to hypnotize me? Because I don't consent to that!"

"Type number three," said Janno, practically bored.

"Are you hypnotizing me or not? I want a straight answer!"

"In a word: no. Nothing of the sort! But congratulations, your argument about self-hypnosis is a new one! I've never heard that one before. In this one regard, you are exceptional."

"You'll see that I am exceptional in every regard—let's bet on it. Assuming that I am not hypnotized by you, or in any other way hindered in my motion, I will, through the strength of my own will power, do something at time X discernibly different than what we have seen me do in advance. What do you say?"

"That all the others have spoken in just the same way, and with just the same confidence. They always think that their will is enough to pull it off. As if they hadn't already learned that lesson."

They turned into the orange corridor, and Janno reached for a picture hanging in the archway and turned it around. The picture showed the great Enlightenment thinker Christian Wolff, smiling optimistically, and on the back was printed:

By this point, everyone has offered a bet

"A cheap trick," said the visitor. "If I hadn't offered the bet, you wouldn't have touched the picture. And what's with all these gimmicks, anyway?" he went on. "All that's missing is a ghost, and we'll be at Simon the magician's. I find this sort of behavior, shall we say, not up to scientific standards. And that's putting it mildly."

"Think of it as gallows humor," said Janno bitterly. "It's necessary; it makes the helplessness bearable. It's a bit shabby, you're right about that. It's all a little run down, but there's nothing for it. I'm not really disagreeing with you at all."

He hung the picture back up and said: "Nevertheless, I'd say you are very likely a type five."

"What's that: type five?"

"Your closing argument. I'm only telling you now since you complained that I'm only showing what I know after the fact."

"What, do you have a catalog of the types?"

"Of course. Pavlo can show it to you. It is very interesting from a psychological point of view: the taxonomy of denial. Type one questions the accuracy of the instrument. For example: someone is sitting at the table and says, 'so, now I'll stand up!' but just then passes the moment at which he had seen himself sitting, and he explains that the clock must be off. Type two is the one who sees that he is going to scratch his head, and says: 'I will not do that!' but just as he is speaking, scratches his head in the precise way and at the precise time that he had seen. He swears, and says that he was tricked—that comes close to your hypothesis of self-hypnosis. Type three, then, the hypnosis theory proper . . ."

"Allow me: is impossible to refute, at least for the experimental subject."

Janno shrugged his shoulders silently. They turned into the red corridor.

"Pavlo's lab is at the end, practically in the infrared, we like to say."

The visitor asked whether the colours of the doors ran in the opposite direction as everywhere else. When Janno explained that the colours were the same as always, corresponding to security classifications, starting with red and going up from there, the visitor said he was astonished that Janno was in the blue corridor, and thus considerably higher than Pavlo, when it seemed like Janno only collected newspaper clippings, whereas . . .

"Precisely. The past is the tricky thing; the future is still untouched. That is," he added quickly, "we're all little people here, it's just an orange institute."

"The same as logic," growled the visitor. Then, abruptly sticking out his hand: "What do you say, do you take the bet or not? I'll put up five pounds against one!"

"I can't do that," protested Janno. "I know for a fact that you will lose. No, don't interrupt, let me finish. Pavlo has done this hundreds of times, and I have been there for dozens of them, and there has not been a single exception—not one! We see: the subject is sitting sideways in the chair, twenty seconds in the future—and immediately he stands up and starts running madly around the room, smashes his ankle and falls back into his chair sideways, exactly at the time he was supposed to. It happens a second time: this time he is going to be sitting at the table, after, say, eighteen seconds. It's the same subject as before, and once again he stands up, but this time he walks slowly, since, he says, that was a one-time thing, there's no way he'll smash his foot again! And so he walks slowly along the table, then, suddenly with no explanation he says, 'you think I'm going to play along with this, and do whatever you want?" And he sits down and growls, 'I have my own free will after all!' Naturally, he is sitting at just the moment we saw. We were in shock, him most of all, because he'd become fixated, and made a theory out of his failure. He was done acting the way other people wanted, he explained, and from now on he would obey *only* his own free will and thus constitute himself as an individual. The elections for the head of the institute were about to happen. He sat down and wrote a letter to the central committee to the effect that he refused to vote for any of the candidates, but, of all the damn twists, nearly everyone wrote a similar letter, and the top candidate got withdrawn by order from the very top—it was the case of the supposedly corrupt X X, if you recall, where it turned out later that the charges were all false. Instead of wising up, our free-willed hero just dug himself deeper and deeper: first, out of personal spite, he defies something utterly reasonable, and every single other person does the same thing; then he does something obviously stupid, and everyone imitates him. Soon it becomes the law of the institution, and it was actually one that the leadership had not dared to introduce for a long time, even though they had wanted to and had been given clearance from above to do so. Finally he sees one way to prove his free will, and out of nowhere he kills himself—and on the same day a suicide epidemic breaks out! He sure savored his helplessness. It must have had an uncanny attraction!"

"Pah, self-hypnosis, nothing more," the visitor scoffed; and: he raised the bet to ten-against-one.

Finally they came to a stop in front of Pavlo's lab.

"We're not idiots," Janno said darkly, "even if we're only an orange institute! We have brought psychologists; we tied one subject to the chair when we saw that he would stand up, and then he had an allergic reaction to the plastic cords, and an attack of itching drove him up into the air. We wanted to try it with steel chains, but then the man started only seeing a tenth of a second into the future, and finally he categorically refused to experiment further. He said it was giving him nightmares. I could tell you hundreds of cases like that. We have filmed the whole process, determined time-X to the microsecond, and always the same thing, every time: the future happens exactly as it happens. What was seen in the blue light comes to pass, and there's no escaping it and no changing it. 'Crazy,' you say, but soon you feel like the crazy one; you laugh first, but it laughs last, and it is a hellish laughter, toying with you. And there's nothing you can do; you can't do anything—believe me, it's unimaginable!"

"I have a powerful imagination," said the visitor.

"But not about this! Trust our experience! We felt it already the very first time: the embarrassment and the despair. Spare yourself, I beg you! I am your friend, and I'm telling you again—"

"And," said the visitor, his hand on the knob of Pavlo's office door, "do you have an explanation? You do have a degree in causality. No cause without an effect, at least that's how you teach it, just like the comrade classics say. So how do you explain it?"

"AC-attraction," said Janno softly.

"What's that—AC?"

"Anti-causality," he began, but just then a shout—"God damn it!"—sounded from behind the door. "If you're coming in, get on with it! I'm sick of this same routine in front of the door."

The visitor walked in and stood meekly near the door. Janno pushed him forwards. The laboratory was a roomy cell that looked like a laundry room: cement walls, cement floor, cement ceiling; a narrow cement window, narrow streams of vapor from the booze, and smoke. No picture on the wall, no flowers, not even a board with blue and red statistical curves, and no colours at all except for grey. Even the desk, and Pavlo sitting behind it, were grey: brown-grey and ash-grey, respectively, and between the desk and the window stood—the only machine of any sort in the room—a white-grey stool with a bowl made of grey-white plastic, and in front of it, there stood the lumpy black-grey outline of a chair.

Pavlo snorted like a walrus, and his bloated, stubbly skull arose from the depths of his seat. He put something in the drawer of the desk and slid it closed with his forearm. His gaze was vacant.

The visitor was still standing on the threshold.

"This is Pavlo," said Janno.

Pavlo wheezed; the visitor took a step towards him, and Janno cried out.

"I'll be damned!" he cried. "The computer!"

"You, sir, stay put," shouted Pavlo at the same time.

The visitor stayed put.

"Oh matter!" said Janno, "I've never seen that before before."

The visitor, looking for the computer, followed the gazes of both scientists and contemplated the stool carefully. A washing-bowl was positioned at waist height on the stool: four truncated cones made of tin for feet; on top, on the circular tin edge, the plastic bowl, and halfway up, where normally a sheet for soda and sand would be, stood a green-grey little box the size of a manicure set, which was attached by two silver-grey wires to a control board on the desk, which had five knobs. Between the bowl and the box the visitor noticed two strings as thin as hairs, glistening in the light of the grey cement, and finally he thought he also noticed on the face of the computer—if this was the computer, which it was—a dial with the faintly visible line of a needle, but no other details. Nothing gave him any sense of what the two had meant with their shouts.

"Green," said Janno thoughtfully, "green. And it holds steady . . . steady . . . steady."

Pavlo stood bent over the desk, his vacant gaze fixed on the line on the dial. "Take a step closer," he ordered with a snort, "but just one step."

Obediently, the visitor took a step closer to the desk with the wash-stand.

"I think the loop is still expanding," said Janno, and as he spoke it seemed to the visitor that the needle was edging a touch farther into the green. But it could have been a trick, since Pavlo had flipped something on the second-to-last knob on the control board, and at that moment a blind descended over the window and the light along the edges of the ceiling came on, leaving everything bathed in a cold glow.

Janno, who had taken from a hook near the door an asbestos Ku-Klux-Klan smock that covered him completely except for two eye-slits, knelt on one knee in front of the computer. "Really, nine-eight, that is unbelievable!"

Pavlo held his walrus skull in his hands.

"You, do you have any printed materials with you?" he asked the visitor. "Any old paper books, little pictures, anything like that?"

The visitor explained that he only had his personal ID and his logician's credentials, and of course the numbered marker on his back, and Pavlo explained that those wouldn't make any difference. "But some printed things," he went on, "especially old ones, often have more of an effect on our computer than the human subject, and that is terribly irritating. You think you're going to see far into the future in the blue light, but then you don't see anything at all—the loop was made by some book or something. But a book's got no eyes, and we don't know any way for it to see. You really don't have anything? Not even a letter?"

The visitor thought for a moment and said that he did not.

"Photographs?"

The visitor cleared his throat in embarrassment: "So, you know, speaking man to man," he was about to make a confession, but Pavlo saved him the embarrassment. "Don't worry, *those* don't have any effect either. As long as they're not old."

Relieved, he shook his head.

"Nine point nine," reported Janno. "Your AC quotient is fabulous! I've never seen such stability—maybe you really are exceptional."

His voice sounded muffled under his hood. The visitor, in his regular clothes, turned to the hook on the door, but it was empty.

"You don't need a suit," Pavlo assured him. "It's just protection for the computer. Otherwise the aura you give off when you look into the future would be distorted by us office workers. Don't worry, nothing will happen to you!"

"And you, Mr. Pavlo, do you need any protection?"

Janno gave his first untroubled laugh. You could even hear it through his hood.

"Him?" he said cavalierly, pointing a finger at his colleague, "he's paralyzed by schnapps! Completely dulled, you understand, really out of it. Not a single second of the future would be bending his way—he's practically a part of the machine. But come one step closer."

The visitor did as he was told, and Janno exclaimed in joy: "Ten minutes! O matter, a full ten minutes! A dream record, and it's holding firm! What an AC attraction! What a loop! It doesn't get any bigger than this!"

"Have you explained to him how it works?" asked Pavlo.

"We were just talking about AC when you started swearing at us. You explain it to him; you're the experimental director, after all."

"I am a simple practitioner," grumbled Pavlo. "All the theory I've got can be summed up in seven words, or in twelve if you want me to be really explicit. You explain it, you theoretical luminary! I can see how much you want to!"

"So," Janno spoke from under the hood: "AC, anticausality, the anti-causal nexus—how should I put it? You know that many phenomena of nature and society have an opposing structure, an anti: bodies and antibodies, capital and anti-capital, reforms and antireforms, eroticism and anti-eroticism, spirit and anti-spirit. Causality works the same way. AC is simply the reversal of the usual nexus."

"So, effect without cause," offered the visitor.

"Oh no," Janno replied with pedagogical eagerness. "That would be some natural first cause. Even the opposite of that, cause without effect, that is, special cultural phenomena, even particular decisions, is not at issue here, even if it does exist. Both of these appearances are not anti-, they are only acausality, simply a rejection of the causal, expressed with the word 'without.' But anti-causality doesn't negate the causal relationship, it reverses it; it does not set it equal to zero but turns its plus into minus and its minus into plus. Just as anti-matter is the reverse of normal matter: a negative nucleus instead of positive, positive electron instead of negative. So anti-causality would be –"

"—a reversed causal nexus," the visitor continued, "but wouldn't that depend on the effect preceding and being the reason for the cause?"

"Exactly, my good logician," said Janno. "To put it precisely: the causal relation in the case of anti-causality is structured so that what we normally call the effect, that is, the later event, is in fact the cause of that which preceded it, what in the usual nexus would be called the cause."

"Ha," interjected the visitor, now no less enthusiastic than his opponent. "All you've done is to switch the names! Otherwise it couldn't be possible. I'll stomp my foot, it makes a sound"—he did so, and it did—"and now I take the cause, the stomp, and say that it's the effect, and take the effect, the sound, and call it the cause. I have changed the terms, but the process itself is the same as before!"

He stomped again; it made the same sound.

"Stomp, sound: cause, effect. Stomp, sound: effect, cause. Does this change anything in reality?" And he stomped a third time, and the sound rang out for the third time.

"If it were just a bit of hocus-pocus," said Janno, "then it would be foolish to play around with it, but AC is reality. AC is not a renaming. AC is a process in reality, just as anti-matter exists objectively, not only in theory. AC exists, there's no doubt about it, just as there is no doubt that its attraction is getting stronger. Your example is a bit tricky, but since you brought it up: in an AC nexus, we would say your foot stomps because a future sound has compelled it to do so. The sound would be the actual cause, not just in name, but in reality, and therefore appropriately placed in the future; and the stomping would be the actual effect, and it really does precede its cause."

"Too complicated!" Pavlo wheezed. "Much too complicated." Leaning over the table, he began to tremble. A bottle from the drawer; he drank, and his visitor, smelling the fumes, thought: what cheap swill!

"But that's absurd," he said, repressing a wave of disgust, to Janno. "I mean, all that with the stomp and the sound."

Pavlo put the bottle back.

"Of course it's absurd. That's why it's AC," answered Janno. "AC is absurd, but it is also real. Still, your example is an odd one. The example that will finally convince you is still coming . . . " And softly, hardly audible under his hood, he added: "unless you really are exceptional."

"Of course," he continued after a pause, which his visitor used to think it over, "of course the normal rule of the nexus applies here, so a *post hoc* does not necessarily mean a *propter hoc*; but it's reversed; an *ante hoc* does not necessarily mean a *propter hoc*. And one more thing: it would be a mistake to believe that AC is a universally obtaining relationship, just as it's a mistake to believe that only the past determines the present. AC is not the only principle, it's probably not even the dominant principle. But it exists *too*, and the *too* is the terrible part. It is the attraction of future events that has its part in determining what happens today. The mouth of an octopus with invisible tentacles, and we're being pulled towards it. We believe that we have free will, and we look toward the future that doesn't exist yet, but which can still be a cause of what we do in the present."

"Excuse me," said the visitor, "but that is unprovable. Whatever you say, as far as I'm concerned it comes down to a simple renaming. How could you prove that the later thing is the cause? First the stomping, then the sound—that's true with or without your AC. You would never be able to prove that I or my foot is stomping because the sound exists in the future. I can still explain it in the usual way: I stomp, it makes a sound: cause and effect, and if you want to change the names, that's a pointless game. It has nothing to do with science."

"The criterion for judging," said Janno, "is how it works in practice. You still have not seen all that happens in this room, things which cannot be explained otherwise."

"But you have told me about it, and that is enough to see that cause and effect are at work, and there's nothing mystical about it. One person hit his foot and therefore fell down into the chair—"

"—but he did not want to sit, understand! He was working against it, and he was forced into it! That he would sit, would definitely sit, that was the future cause, and his stumbling was the effect, and admittedly the way it came to pass was not completely determined by its cause. But its essence, that is, that he would end up sitting, was determined in advance."

"Pah, self-hypnosis, nothing more." The visitor punched the air with his fist. "He was self-conscious, and that caused him to trip."

"But see, that also supports my theory! What is responsible for the self-hypnosis? What is responsible for his self-consciousness? It was what he had seen. And what he had seen was demonstrably in the future, it was the later event, and as such it was the cause of an effect that lay before it in the course of time. You can call it self-hypnosis if you like—but the main thing is that something later has determined something earlier. That is real AC!"

The visitor paused, then said, "but he saw it before he stumbled."

"Yes, he did see it," said Janno, "his vision came first. But his vision wasn't anything objectively real, it was just a mental image of what was coming. The real event only came later."

"To hell with it . . . " said the visitor.

"Either," the sound came out from under the hood, "you accept this after-and-before, or else fundamentally change your concept of the material world!"

"Much too complicated," said Pavlo, "much too complicated."

"Quite simple," said Janno, "quite simple indeed: AC means: what comes later determines what comes sooner—the future effects the present. I think that is simple enough.

"That's better," said Pavlo, "but it's still a bit overblown."

"And the past?" asked the visitor.

Janno hesitated.

Pavlo took a drink.

"Forgive me," said Janno quietly at last, "but that is confidential—the regulations of the institute, you understand . . . "

"Of course," said the visitor, "I understand that quite well."

He thought for a moment, then asked, half as a declaration, half as a question, "so a kind of teleology?"

"Something related," Janno replied with relief. "Teleology is growth towards a goal, the unfolding of something already fixed; AC is growth from out of something, the unfolding of something still to come, something fixed only in the future and which determines what goes on now. Our grammar doesn't do a good job expressing it. Maybe the best way of putting it would be: anti-teleology."

"Bullshit, I've had enough," said the visitor decisively. "You're floundering around in a net of self-hypnosis and trying to make a theory out of it. I raise the stakes to twenty-to-one."

"Now he's playing Faust," laughed Pavlo. "But will he sign with blood?" After giving a start, the visitor came right back with: "what would you like to bet, vodka coupons?"

"A full pound," said Janno.

The bottle clanked on the table. "Man," said Pavlo, "oh man!"

"We're not allowed to do that," said Janno. "What if he *is* exceptional?"

He stepped back from the console, and suddenly the visitor saw the box, which until then had been hidden from view by Janno. It shone its pure green, gentle, a jewel with the soul of an apple, and all the grey of the room seemed to be nuzzling protectively up to this substance.

"What's your bet?" Pavlo chimed in.

"Ah," said Janno, "the usual hubris, of course. Each pact is always the only one."

"We have warned you, sir!" said Pavlo, reaching his hand over the table. "You will have no grounds for complaint afterwards." But the visitor didn't put his hand in yet.

"You said something about Faust and blood," he said carefully. "What is that supposed to mean? I am, you know, rather sensitive to pain. You didn't mean that you would . . . "

"No, no," Pavlo assured him, "nothing to worry about. That's just an old paper book, completely unscientific, you see, but—well, then."

The visitor still hesitated.

"What'll it be, then?" Pavlo urged him on. "Are you in? You won't feel a thing. You can go ahead and step closer."

The visitor seemed not to notice.

"Good," he said, suddenly happy, as if snapping out of a dream. "Agreed. Twenty-to-one. And now you'll both see that there's no such thing as this ghostly AC! Helplessness—sure, but it'll be your helplessness this time. I declare war on the ghosts of the future!"

"I hope you win," said Janno slowly. "It would disprove my theory, but still—"

Then, firmly, almost shouting, "I hope so!"

His hands separated from one another.

"Have a seat," Pavlo invited.

The visitor went to the console, and now he saw that on the apple-green computer there were two scales with two dials on them. The dial on the larger scale stood all the way to the right, at ten; the needle on the smaller one, which was shaped like a semi-circle and covered in small markings, was twitching around zero.

"Go ahead and take a dunk!" commanded Pavlo.

The visitor took a seat on the chair and sank his head into the bowl. Pavlo attached—and as he did so the visitor looked at him extremely skeptically from the outermost corner of his eye—Pavlo attached a third wire, which he hadn't noticed before, running out from the bowl and taped it to the back of his head. He felt nothing; he saw nothing except the inside of the bowl and, through it, part of the table, but still he was clearly uneasy.

"It won't hurt, don't worry!" Pavlo reassured him. "Just a little buzzing. It's just a bit of a stopgap, I'm sure you understand! We sure could use some real copper, or even real wood for the switchboard, sometimes the buttons stick real bad—but where would we get something nice, anyway? Real wood, no way! We're just an orange institute, and in the red floor at that, no concessions for us. You must know how that is. Logic isn't going to make it past the violet floor either. But our results are still reliable. And now I'll go ahead and strap you in."

From inside the bowl, the visitor checked that he would be seeing ten minutes ahead, and Pavlo confirmed it: Yes, ten minutes, but only the last few seconds of that. How many seconds, we'll see, probably twenty-five to thirty.

"Exceptional," whispered Janno, "exceptional!"

"Rest your head in the bowl, nice and easy, just like that. Twenty whole pounds, and you know that this is being filmed." Pavlo pushed the top button, a light-grey square appeared on the cement wall next to the window.

"Here we go!" said Pavlo, pushing a second button, and the little needle gave a quick jump nearly to the right end of the scale.

"Thirty seconds!" reported Janno.

"All right," said Pavlo, "that's right. You will see thirty seconds. From the moment of activation that will be the thirtieth second of the ninth minute, and you will see precisely until the beginning of the tenth minute."

"No," said Janno. "Until minute nine, the end of second fifty-nine."

"Nonsense, until ten-point-zero-zero."

"Nine fifty-nine point nine nine!"

"Ten-zero-zero!"

"It doesn't matter," sounded from the bowl, "it's all the same! I will repeat my bet once again. If I see myself walking, I will sit down. If I see myself seated, I will walk—that is, whatever is the opposite of what I saw, and I will unambiguously declare beforehand what I am going to do! Now, begin! I am ready!"

"Synchronize the clocks," Janno suggested.

The visitor looked at his wrist through the bottom of the bowl. "Eleven forty-one."

"Right, four seconds to go—three—two—one—zero."

Pavlo pushed the middle button, and with a buzzing sound a flickering blue oval formed over the apple-green bottom of the bowl. The head of the visitor stood out like a giant mythological bust. At the same time there appeared in the square on the cement the shadow of someone walking, seen from the front. Knowing already who it would be, the experts immediately recognized the image coming into focus as their visitor.

"I am walking down the street, down Eichenallee!" called the visitor, who saw himself, with crystal clarity, walking towards himself with a grotesque expression on his face. "I am walking down Eichenallee, so I will say seated here at the table! I will—"

And just then the walking shadow made an abrupt turn in front of a black colossus, revealing over his right shoulder the shaft of a spear sticking out of his back, wobbling from his motion, and as he cried out from inside the bowl, there appeared in the square the blurry and shaky image of the front of a row of buildings, and a window in the fifth floor began to expand.

Something was moving, and again he cried out from inside the blue light: "That's the little Biebls child in the open window!" And the grey and blue form the desperate would-be savior came running, the shaft of a spear dangling from his back. The visitor jumped from his chair. The wire ripped out.

The little needle, marking the twenty-ninth second, stood still, and the large one seemed to do the same, the computer showed only grey. The light in the bowl went out, but the visitor wasn't paying attention.

"A telephone book, do you have a telephone book?" he shouted, and Janno dashed off.

"There's no phone here," Pavlo snarled. "This corridor is only red!" and: "there are only telephone books at the central institutes, and you can't go there anyway."

But immediately the visitor took off after Janno. He saw him open a door in the yellow corridor: "A phone book" said the lab-worker, "you're in luck, we just happen to have one lying around right here!"

The logician ripped the book from his hand. It was the edition from six years ago, but the Biebls were still living in the same place, and he knew the changes in the area codes off hand. The logician dialed; the line was free; the call went through; no one picked up.

Of course: working hours. The line went dead, and soon a busy signal came on.

"That can happen here," said that lab-worker, "when someone from the blue level needs to make a call."

"That makes no sense," said the logician. "Try again, and report it to the fire department. It's the house opposite mine, Eichenallee 98c!"

He ran out of the room.

"Your ID card!" shouted Janno. "Your pass! Otherwise you won't get through!"

The visitor was already gone.

"You still need to enter the time," said the guard as Janno finally caught up to him with his ID card.

"Eleven forty-three," said the logician, sweat on his brow. "Two minutes gone! But it's only three blocks from here, I'll make it!"

The guard read over the document once again, looked at his watch and nodded; he needed a break anyway. The steel door slid up; into the open; to the intersection; red light; cross; a policeman whistles; the pedestrian mover was running perpendicular to his path; no way around it; better wait on the sidewalk: the light can't stay red for more than thirty seconds, it'll be faster to wait for it than to get in trouble with the police! Green; he jumped onto the pedestrian mover; the policeman did the same thing.

"Hey, you" he said, tapping on his helmet. "Just now on red you—"

He kept walking.

"Hey, citizen!" The policeman threw his magnetic reel at the fugitive's back-plate and pulled him back with his microwinder; "hey you, number 17-1-13-OR, just now you tried to cross on red—"

"Let me go!" cried the detained man, "or else the kid is going to fall!"

"What kid?" asked the policeman, opening the memory of his mobile computer, pulling out his notepad just to be safe.

"At Eichenallee 98c, the second window from the left!"

"You can't see that from here!"

"I saw it," gasped number 17-1-13-OR, "at the bottom of the bowl, in the future, in the blue light, please understand!"

"At the bottom of something, I get it," said the policeman, scribbling away and looking at his computer. "Member of the intelligentsia, a lot of money, normal colour, we know! And now, start at the beginning!"

The logician sighed. "Listen, I was at the FS—"

"Where?"

"The institute for the investigation of future structures."

"Aha!" His stylus scraped on his notepad. "And with whom?"

"28-3-74-OB!"

"Which department is that? I know my way around there, so don't try to fool me."

"Registration and information surveillance."

"Earthman, that must be a blue division! Do you have your authorization pass?"

He whistled through his teeth.

"And now in such a hurry," he said slowly.

A despairing glance at the clock: five more minutes. Number 17-1-13-OR hit the policeman hard with the side of his hand on his magnetic reel and landed a blow on his stomach. He went down; the magnetic rod, like a spear stuck in his number plate, wobbled back and forth in the wind. It was as light as a feather. The passersby didn't see, or else looked away.

Green again; the logician ran.

An attack, it occurred to him, an attack on an armed officer is something completely unexpected;

something completely unexpected elicits slow reactions, which means that a slow reaction is among the things caused by my attack, and as this was occurring to him he thought: the Bamalip model! And as he was thinking, it occurred to him: the future is *not* fixed!

Pulling himself together, he thought: nothing else, o God, just don't let this go wrong, the pedestrian mover here is always broken!

The pedestrian mover was rolling without a hitch.

The sidewalk; people rushed and swelled; a siren sounded; a whistling far behind him, and now there's a whistling—a loud one—ahead, too. The girl's auxiliary came down the street, a whole regiment to judge by the sound. Pipes, flutes, recorders, timpani, the beloved march number seven: *Our path goes straight into the morning, and the morning is beautiful and bright!*

The tambourine major twirled the Turkish crescent; the company came to a stop and applauded. O matter, thought the logician, if she throws her baton now, there will be a street concert! The tambourine major threw her baton, the soldiers began marching in place and prepared to turn. The baton took to the air a second time; the timpani sounded; the company turned, and the logician, the magnetic block on his back, wove a path through the uniforms.

A thousand voices rose in outrage; the confused musicians kept marching; one fell down; the crowd raged. On the sidewalk opposite a police captain got his net ready. The siren cried out and then fell silent. It obviously wasn't going to interrupt the concert.

"Comrade people's protector!" cried the logician and ran directly toward the net. "Comrade, don't throw the net. There's a child in danger—on Eichenallee!"

The voice of the logician was so plaintive that the police captain put his net away and stepped out of the way.

"Thank you, comrade!" called 17-1-13-OR, already running. The street to Eichenallee, he knew, was torn open for underground construction; but what he didn't know was that the construction workers, in their eagerness to see the street concert, were removing the footbridges over the construction zone and using them as improvised bleachers. The concert began as always with the national anthem, the recorders grabbed the audience by the heart; the logician climbed through the construction zone. Cables, coal tar, phosphorescents, a gas pipe hissed. He did not take the time to look at his watch.

Not nine minutes and fifty-nine seconds, he said to himself, no, he had ten minutes! One second, that one second! He came to Eichenallee; gasped, ran. —

"He's running," said Pavlo. Janno had come back and they were watching the film of those thirty (or twenty-nine, because of the interruption) seconds, and it was all just as it was now happening in reality. "Of course he's running," grumbled the scholar. "That's what he saw, that he would be running!" The siren, a fire truck; the logician sprang just to the side.—"what gave him such a fright?" asked Pavlo. "That thing in his back, looks like a magnet rod—oh, he's pulled it out, looks like he will be sitting after all. Sitting in a cell."

The logician looked up at the building where the Biebls lived.

On the fifth floor a window opened.

Janno bit his lip.

"The window," said Pavlo, "the window is opening."

A child crept onto the window's edge.

"It's crawling," said Pavlo and grabbed the bottle.

"No!" screamed the logician. "No!" He jumped up, and in bounding strides took off after the fire brigade, who were carefully climbing, with a life net, through a trench that was cut right up to the house door.

The film broke off; abrupt flickering. "Time's up," said Pavlo, and Janno roared back, "you ass, o you ass, you stupid, drunken ass," and then jumped to the wash stand and kicked it into the corner, and stormed out.

"As if that changes anything!" said Pavlo shaking his head, the half-empty bottle at his lips. "As if that changes anything at all! I don't think that Janno will ever figure it out. That's blue corridor thinking, a lot of wishful thinking there . . . "

He pulled the glass shards together with his foot. "You know, you could put his whole AC theory in seven words: 'Not a damn thing you can do.' That's all. And I'll add five more of my own: 'And that machine knows it.'

He could still hear Janno ranting. Pavlo threw the empty bottle into the pile of tin and glass shards in the corner. "What's gonna happen—happens," he repeated softly; then he went to the window and opened it. Eighteenth floor, in the distance a street concert. He heaved himself onto the windowsill; a rush of horror; he fell back.

"It seems unlikely," he said, shocked by the fresh air. His tongue felt swollen. Standing stiff and motionless like a man who is about to fall, he spoke loudly and struggled not to slur his words: "But now I'm really curious to see if he'll make good on the bet!"

And he added, slowly, contemplating a piece of wire: "I would buy a wreath for the kid, I'd spend all the money on it, yes, all of it—" and then, shaking his head, starting to sway: "—all right, maybe half of it" and then he fell back onto the broken computer. In the hallway, Janno's shouting had long since fallen silent.

The Heap

After his friend Janno, the causologist, had not shown his face for five weeks, contrary to his usual habit, the neutrinologist Jirro decided to pay his absent friend a visit at work. He found Janno in the lab, engaged in a strange activity that was hard to reconcile with the usual duties of a causologist.

In a sink in front of the desk and the closet for the lab uniforms, which was how most minor labs were configured in the Institute of Philosophy, lay a heap of small screws. Facing the sink stood a flashing camera mounted on a tripod. As Jirro walked in, he watched Janno take a screw from the bowl, throw it into a shoe box full of more screws under the sink, turn back to the camera, press the shutter release, and then wind the film to the next frame. He greeted Jirro with the pleading look of a desperately overwhelmed man, sighing "Hello", only to reach into the heap in the sink again.

What in the holy matter was he doing?

Working, grumbled Janno, and threw out another screw.

Was he taking an indirect approach to understanding the concept of subtraction? Jirro asked, exasperated.

"Actually it's the other way around," Janno replied, throwing another screw into the box. He took another snapshot of the perhaps 500-strong heap of objects, now diminished by three.

How many exactly were in this heap, inquired the visitor, and barely had he spoken the words when he felt himself grabbed by the arm and swung around.

"It *is* a heap, isn't it?" asked Janno, almost helpless.

"Of course. A heap of screws. No wonder everyone's short of screws!" Jirro said in a tone of annoyance. "Poor Pavlo can't locate the ten screws he needs for his new invention, a time turner, and you're just messing around with them here! Next you're going to tell me they're genuine steel screws too!!"

"They're real", replied Janno.

Jirro took a closer look. "Holy Matter, they *are* steel screws!"

He wanted to count out ten of them for Pavlo, but Janno protested: "Those have been budgeted and accounted for, don't make trouble! Orders from the philosopher-in-chief, highest priority!"

His visitor whistled through his teeth: A new line of command? The highest orders rarely came through the Institute of Philosophy, but you never know.—"Earthman, will you explain already!" he urged him.

Janno's face was easy to read; Jirro was surprised to see how he struggled to gather his thoughts, wrenched away from the task at hand. Especially for a pure practitioner. Yet the visitor got the sense that Janno was actually doing this task for himself.

The causologist took a fourth screw from the heap and asked Jirro a question, taking a brief break from his photos only when Jirro answered "vaguely". Did Jirro remember the History of Philosophy, the old Greeks, the Eleatics, their discovery of dialectics? That's when Jirro answered "vaguely" in such a dismissive tone that Janno, screw between his fingers, decided just to tell the story behind his assignment.

In recent weeks, the country had become embroiled in yet another battle of convictions, in an attempt to prove how the ideal character of real society, which is not always visible in everyday life, is the true subject of the social ideal. These attempts drew several leaders of domestic and consciousness policy into the pulpit, including the new philosopher-in-chief. However, as Jirro was aware, the latter had until recently been responsible for organizing a number of highly successful special task forces, to great acclaim. He was new to the philosophical front, so he could certainly and understandably not yet be fully acquainted with the intricacies of this difficult terrain. This lack of insight—and now Janno finally threw the screw into the shoe box and took a photo—this lack of insight had caused the philosopher-in-chief to give an unfortunate answer to a disrespectful question from an audience member at one of the debates. Asked whether the prediction of the comrade classics that all existing philosophical dilemmas would be solved by the Truly Free Society had come true, the only prudent answer would have been an all-encompassing "insofar as possible". Instead, he answered "absolutely, positively, fully!" Which was in and of itself correct in its anticipation of the solutions, yet ultimately still somewhat inexact. In fact, hard-pressed by a follow-up question from this same audience member about where exactly the register of solutions could be viewed, he allowed the answer to be drawn out of him that the register was already in print and would appear in one of the upcoming issues of the relevant journal, the "Polemic for Philosophical Certainty". This is the point where Janno finally arrived at the explanation of his, certainly rather curious, task. Much to the confusion of Jirro, Janno now threw the fifth screw he had grabbed not into the shoe box but back into the sink and began walking back and forth between the sink and the desk, all the while still recounting events as though he were performing a demented one-man play; oblivious to the irony of his zealous lecture, now imitating the furious philosopher-in-chief, now as involuntary persiflage of all schools of philosophy. After the debate, the philosopher-in-chief had demanded a copy of the register of resolved philosophical dilemmas which he had not only claimed was real, but which was now actually believed to be real. Repeating his recently completed intensive course in the philosophy of history, he had ventured to hastily manufacture a document—as of course one did not exist. After stumbling onto gaping holes in every area, not just with the old Sophists, but also with the Ionians and Pythagoreans, the Platonists, the Peripatetics, the Stoics, Cynics, Orphists, Gnostic, Patrists, Scholasticists, Empiricists, Skeptics, and other agnostics like the rationalists, irrationalists, sensualists, spiritualists, the (of course!) mechanical materialists, and subagnostics, he, the philosopher-in-chief, bristling with rage, had given the strictest order that the complete and definitive register of solutions was to be delivered by the end of the quarter. He had personally divided the unresolved dilemmas of four thousand years among the Institute's various departments, with the Causality Department receiving the combined sophistry of the Eleates, Megarians, and similar fallacists, while he, Janno, had been assigned the vexatious heap problem of the gentlemen Zeno and Eubulides, with which even Hegel had wrestled, the so-called *sorites* paradox. In simple terms, this problem could be imagined something like this:

The question is what a heap is. For example, a heap of wheat or rice grains or even—and now Janno had returned to the sink and laid his screw almost tenderly onto the valuable stash—or even, as here, a heap of screws: These two are not yet a heap, these three aren't either, not even these four, whereas, as Jirro now ascertained for himself, these five hundred and sixty two are clearly a heap, which raises the question: how many exactly constitute a heap? Or: at how many units would a not-yet-heap begin to be a heap? Or also: at what point would a heap vanish into a state of not-yet-heapdom, which was to say, when would it become equivalent to a not-yet-heap? This *sorites* paradox appeared to be solvable in two ways, namely in the augmentation from not-yet-heap to heap, or in the reduction from heap to no-longer heap, the second method of which he, Janno, was currently expl-

And then, as the philosopher, now demonstrating, tried to take a fifth screw from the basin for the second time, the physicist abruptly interrupted him: Everything was sufficiently clear to him now, he just had one question: who was paying for the massive amounts of film that Janno was exposing? When Janno confessed that he was paying for it himself, since the official inventory of the Institute of Philosophy had run out of film long ago, Jirro shook his head vigorously: That was terrible precedent Janno was introducing here: A causologist, of all people, surely understood the potential consequences of such insanity: If leadership, as was to be expected, were to hear about this terrible precedent, every low level scientist would end up being pressured to fund research costs from their own wallet, with Janno to thank, that much was certain! Janno, now cast from the realm of abstract problems into the everyday, let the screw fall back into the sink and asked, helplessly: "So what am I supposed to do?"

The screws gleamed in the dented sink.

Solve this, what did you call it, *sowrites* paradox without bankrupting your colleagues, Jirro answered impassively, and in response to the stalwart objection that it couldn't be done, be insisted: It had to be done.

"Let me explain to you-", urged Janno, looking at the experimental heap, speaking in that complaisant tone again which all workers at the consciousness institute subconsciously adopted when dealing with applied scientists, and which Jirro couldn't stand, "Let me explain to you –"; and he explained: more than three thousand times had he increased the heap by a single screw at a time, yet each time, the definitive threshold at which the not-yet heap took on the new quality of a heap had been elusive. When he diligently kept his eye on the sink to catch that moment of transition, adding screw to screw, all he could see were the individual elements among a slowly growing number of elements.

Eight, nine, ten, or even seventeen: they remained individual screws and never turned into a heap. Yet as soon as he allowed his weary eyes, in pain from staring, to wander off for a moment, it seemed to him as though, the moment they were trained on the sink again, the united elements suddenly confronted him as a heap. So a clear threshold—which was the sole object of his interest—never appeared in the objectivity of a defined quantity, but rather only through subjective experience of the degree of fatigue in his eyes, which set in between seven and twenty-one screws, a rather wide range. This realization had forced him to find a new way to fix the moment in an objective way that fully excluded any subjective factors, which required film, since this could only be accomplished through photography. Or did his friend have a better suggestion? Jirro answered in the affirmative: Yes, as a matter of fact.

Janno laughed incredulously, which Jirro found rather impertinent, but the desperate hope concealed within that laughter eluded him. What would his friend, he asked with a slowly widening grin, be willing to fork out for that?

Janno let go of his screws, carefully pulling up his pant legs with the laser-sharp creases and sat down in front of the research protocol lying on the creaky desk: Was Jirro talking about a solution to the problem of getting more film, or the problem as a whole?

Jirro laughed, blunt yet genial: Once again it was clear how the gentlemen scholars in the humanities, who take a condescending view of their colleagues working in primary matter as 'unspiritual ninnies', how those scholars in the humanities casually lumped together methods from entirely incompatible categories as though they were similar in nature. Financing research through an employee's private means is not a problem to be solved, let alone an abstract one. That is something that stands outside all manner of debate; an annoyance that should be dealt with on the spot. And since it's become pretty clear that this *sowrites* paradox can't be tackled in any empirical way except through photography, it should be tackled in a non-empirical way. That is, we must chase down the solution in a speculative or conceptual manner (or did the comrade philosopher know a third method?), and once again he asked his friend what he would be willing to pay for a solution.

Janno was of two minds: There was no doubt that Jirro was right. The leaders would be happy to latch on to this initiative, since the photo protocol could never be submitted officially; on the other hand, the deadline loomed. But did Jirro truly know a way? And what should he offer?

He furtively gauged his friend: Was Jirro genuinely in a bind, or did he simply need money, the way those who are chronically underpaid often simply need money? Three pounds, four pounds, five pounds, six pounds, what was his price?

Jirro could see how Janno agonized over the decision, and he stared at him unabashedly, how his friend sat there bent over his protocol, and Jirro brazenly assessed the situation out loud: Things seemed to be going well for his friend. A brand new tie coveted by all; its silver gray contrasting so provocatively against the ashen gray of the lab coat; shoes with real leather tips; a matt bronze luxury version of his ID pin on his lapel and back, and now this ridiculous business of funding his own research. One couldn't help but wonder, had Janno perhaps won the lottery? Seven correct numbers out of seven thousand, a secret hidden even from his best friend?

Janno raised his hands in protest, appalled. No, no, what was his friend insinuating? Just a little logistic moonlighting, the usual, but for some higher ups, and so with considerably higher pay; a bit of information harmonization and the development of dialectic links between "either" and "or", just the same sort of things he did for his bosses every day. These endless privileges of the gentlemen in the Humanities, grumbled Jirro. Physicists are never offered anything like that, so it was about time his friend helped him out. And since Janno, wavering between three and four pounds, remained silent, Jirro named his price: Twenty pounds!

Janno cried out: "Ten is all I've got!"

The neutrinologist moved towards the door and nonchalantly stopped right before he reached it: "Twelve now, the rest on your next payday!"

Groaning; his hand moved to the latch; Janno acquiesced with a nod; "and" demanded Jirro, "ten screws for Pavlo . . . "

Janno turned pale.

But they've been counted and budgeted, he stammered, yet Jirro countered: his friend's dogged refusal was pathetic, he could just write them off, surely a suitable explanation could be found, and as the hinge began to squeak, Janno finally gave in.

His decision seemed to have changed him; perhaps the physicist had said something that had caused a moral elementary particle to jump into a new orbit. "Alright", he said almost cheerfully. He slapped his hand down onto the stack of protocol papers and pushed himself away from the desk, vigorously bouncing back to the sink, where Jirro was already counting out screws from the shoe box. And there, in the washed-out gray cement, over the twinkling of dead matter, he stretched his body the way his awareness stretched, preparing to finally unravel itself.

"The *sorites* solution!" he demanded.

Jirro, his treasure already in his breast pocket, sat down next to the protocol papers.

If, he began obnoxiously slowly and with an indulgent laugh, as if begging for Janno's agreement. If he remembered correctly, their comrades the classical authors differentiated between two qualities of truth: an all-encompassing, all-containing, complete and total truth, which could, however, only be reached by humanity at the end of an eternally stretching path of evolution, and a partial, fragmentary, particular one, which ever-more-precisely approximates totality in the course of human development. And such a partial truth—or in other words, a partial solution, could, yes should, be claimed for the *sorites* as well, since humanity won't last for eternity and such a partial solution already exists. Namely, that five hundred and sixty two screws constitute a heap. And with a grotesque: "Well, what do you say!" Jirro slapped his own thigh.

"Almighty matter", Janno exclaimed, bursting with overwhelming rapture, and Jirro, caught up in the rigor of his own rhetorical thought, guided his mental gymnastics to their conclusion like a march of triumph: A problem, which could be fully resolved with reference to the classics, a problem for which a partial solution exists, is in principle already as good as solved: A partial solution proved the possibility to a total solution, which necessitated the existence of a complete solution, given enough time to find it. So one could report the problem as essentially resolved, and then retire to a life unburdened by the search for its final solution, and with an envious: "Oh citizen, I wish I had it that good just for once!" Jirro rested his case.

Janno, lost in thought, noticed for the first time how unbelievably dirty the window was, slimy gray traces of raindrops, spattered with mortar and bird droppings, never cleaned since he had begun working here, and yet he saw it for the first time and it became a filter for his thoughts, which filled with this heavenly blue, uncanny light that made matter gleam. As he stared at the window and fell back on his usual, proven methods by tracing back Jirro's thoughts, a strong desire washed over him to flood his laboratory with soap suds, bucket after bucket of boiling lye, the floor, the walls, the surfaces, the desk, the stand with the dented, filth-lined sink, in which the screws blossomed like a crystal flower, and he couldn't have said why he wished for this, in fact, he didn't even grasp it as a wish. It simply happened to him, and then it was over. Only the filter of a washed-out blue remained, and in front of it, like a cracking scroll, the abrupt ending of the unspooling of the conclusion, and then, sobered up, Janno saw Jirro.

It can't be done, he said in a flat voice, and in response to Jirro's amazed, uninhibited "why?": "It's a logical leap, isn't it? How am I supposed to prove any of this?"

Jirro sensed what Janno meant, but nevertheless asked: "Prove what?"

"That five hundred and sixty two screws make a heap!"

His friend, not yet worried about his twenty pounds, but still a little concerned (at least there was no way he was giving back the screws) casually brushed it off: "Anyone would agree!"

Janno reiterated: "That's the problem, my friend! Don't you think there'd be unforeseeable consequences? Since when do we allow definitions to be determined through polls? If just anyone can determine what makes a heap, then we might as well let anybody determine what truth is, or justice, or welfare, or—"

and Janno quietly said, finishing his thought, what Jirro was thinking at the same moment: "Or the Truly Liberated Society!"

"Adieu, my pounds!" Jirro thought, but immediately he jumped up from the desk in the middle of the lab, inspired by the brilliance of this place. The two men stood facing each other, diagonally across from the sink and the camera, like two living corners and two inanimate corners of a parallelogram, under the murky blue light from the window.

Buoyed by the prospect of a solution, Jirro confirmed that "just anybody" obviously wouldn't work, as that would set a precedent for the misinterpretation of liberation, which no leader would allow; so—and now he raised his voice –

"So-?"

“So-” now falling back into his triumphant march: “So it can’t be ‘just anybody’!”

Was he expecting the comrade-in-chief (the ultimate “not-just-anybody”) to speak out on such a question, asked Janno? No, certainly not, *he* had other things to worry about, but the comrade classics on the other hand . . .

“Come on, Jirro”; Janno interrupted him. That’s the first thing he’d tried! Of course he’d run the idea through all the classical theories and positions, every single one, and not just their philosophical manuscripts. Yet nowhere had any of them weighed in on the *sorites* paradox, not even the sophists. There was truly not a single usable citation.

Jirro was all too familiar with Janno’s proficiency to doubt his word, so he redirected his perseverance: If no directly suitable citation could be found, then an indirectly suitable one should be used!

And before Janno could open his mouth, he added: You need to look up where the word “heap” has been connected to a concrete number; surely this had come up in the military. There had to be phrases like “a heap of this many mercenary soldiers” in the—

And Janno, heaving a sigh, walked past Jirro, pulled the bottom record from the stack of protocol papers and handed it to him: “Here you go, the complete, alphabetically ordered (of course) register of the uses of the lexeme ‘heap’ in the works of classical authors." Janno read out loud, and Jirro listened: "'Like a heap of vultures the maligned threw themselves –', 'a small heap of adventurers could never–'; 'a heap of "woe-is-me's" leads to nothing-'; 'a heap of addresses doesn't make an organized system'; (followed by forty two variations on the same expression, including 'pile', 'mass' and 'bunch') 'a shabby bunch of officers'; 'what a bunch of clueless-'; 'a mass of pig-headed academics-' (three times); 'this heap of brave Nubian freedom fighters who perished-'"

"Stop!" Jirro interrupted, "stop, that's it!" A third triumph march? Jirro gave it up; he honed his ideas, concisely like a beam of light in the prism of his spectrum: this comment about the Nubian battle for independence referred to a concrete nameable and datable event (Janno nodded). The details suggested a military battle, so it must be possible to reconstruct the exact headcount of this lost heap from the data; there had to have been, at least on the side of the colonial forces, battalion diaries, battle reports, torture protocols, and documents about quantities of ammunition used, which would allow them to draw conclusions, and if, as could be assumed, there was indeed a heap of dead soldiers, then there must be bones to be found, a mass grave in proximity to the site of the battle. All of this could be researched and analyzed, programmed into the computer, and eventually they would be able to declare the exact size of that heap as the partial solution to the *sorites* paradox, which in itself was already the complete solution. Of course that was more than one person alone could accomplish, it would take a broad team: a professional archeologist, two or three forensic doctors, a carefully selected historicist, about eight or nine assistant sociologists and finally Janno to lead this task force, which could definitely mean a move into a higher income bracket for him; add a work trip to the Sahara and—(and since Janno looked ready to interrupt him again, Jirro raised his voice; while he was not quite singing his third march of triumph yet, he had reached the level of an exulted hymn): And shining brightly across these victories would be their friendship, which, a neutrino of true ethics, would endure into the matter of the most distant future. He, Jirro, solemnly vowed not to raise the price of his solution, even though he ought to do. He would be happy to settle for the agreed-upon twenty pounds, the first twelve of which, however, would be due immediately—

He reached out with an open hand, and Janno grabbed it, and so they stood across from the devices, and after nothing had happened for a while, Jirro stated that this handshake, which sealed their pact, could endure forever as a symbol, but he would eventually need to get back to work, and so could Janno take care of the first installment now? And Janno, laughing with a sense of nervous desolation, slowly let go of his friend's hand, looked out the window, and said: "Oh dear!"—What: Oh dear?

"This isn't the true solution!"

Jirro was speechless.

He was his friend, said Janno, looking intently at the window, as though a message was materializing from the figures in the grime. He was his friend, and so he would confess what he couldn't admit to anyone else: This improvised reasoning certainly sounded convincing, a masterstroke of implicational art, yet if Janno hadn't completed the same reasoning long ago then only because he . . . as he . . . since he had a hunch—

He stumbled, disconcerted by his use of such unscientific terms, but the strained light working its way through the window put a twinkle in his eye.

Jirro looked worried.

"I want the real solution!" Janno exclaimed; suddenly he was crying; "don't you get it, the real solution, the solution to the problem!"

Jirro, suddenly shivering, forced himself to calm down: they wouldn't have installed listening devices in minor laboratories like this, surely! Still, quick look: No pictures on the walls: good! No telephone: good! The window was closed: matter be praised!—After the outburst, his friend stood softly wheezing, hands flying—that was good too: Nothing worse than the calm composure that preceded a storm of unforeseeable proportions. Still, even a meltdown carried plenty of risk, and different kinds of risks, that much was certain!

Keeping a close eye on his friend, Jirro took the brain probe out of his bag, that pencil-sized consciousness detector, which was standard equipment for any researcher of second rank or higher, but Janno shoved him back.

"What are you thinking! There's nothing wrong with me!" Jirro retracted the whirring hair probe, and said, dropping the device back into its holster: "Lord of Matter, calm down, calm down, that's how things started in physics once too, and generations later we're still paying the price for what happened! Our ancestors from Galileo to Einstein spent three hundred years looking only for real solutions, the solutions to their problems, nothing else, and what did that get us? Well, we know the answer: two nuclear wars and our ostracized from the rest of the world, and ever since, parents have warned their kids: You better be industrious and tidy, or you'll be forced to volunteer to study physics! Ever since, a comrade from the freedom-monitoring troops sits in every laboratory and waits, so that we can discover more things we already know, every single time: something we already know, and believe me, that's the way things ought to be! I'm sorry I'm giving you such an elementary lecture, but you really went off the rails! You want to research the *sorites* paradox for its own sake, instead of providing the proof so that the predictions of the comrade classics can be fulfilled in this respect (since that's the point of your assignment)—do you understand what will come of your egoism in the end? You don't, so let me tell you: This is how the atomic bomb started, exactly like this, with this very question: When does quantity become quality, when does a quantity of peacefully existing material become a combustible mass? This 'critical mass' of the qualitative leap—there's your heap paradox! You take a plutonium atom, that good Plutonium 239, take an atom, and another and another, and it's still not a critical mass, but then suddenly comes one more atom that pushes it over the line: there's no photographing that.—Fine, it won't happen exactly like that with your screws. The atomic nuclei of iron can't spontaneously disintegrate, yet this *sorites* paradox is worse than the plutonium one: with an atomic bomb, we knew what would happen, but think about it: When you add screw to screw, yet you're not just piling screw upon screw, you're also piling thought upon thought and desire upon desire and ultimately trouble upon trouble and you think you're moving in the realm of philosophy, when in reality you've long ventured into the realm of social ethics! Your *sorites* paradox can *also* turn explosive, a sociopolitical bomb, and with your theory it's *already* become one: You're blasting society into the nothingness of a no-longer calculable future! Freedom is insight into what's necessary, I'm sorry, every child knows that, but you're still trying to annihilate the necessary, the orientation of all prescient thinking, preserved for the benefit of society, yet by destroying the necessary you also blow up freedom, and that is not our prerogative!"

And quietly now, friend to friend: "Get yourself tested! You can do it yourself! When you produce an appropriate conscientiogram, with a couple of nice surges in cloudiness, you can spend a few weeks in a sanatorium, in the mountains, or even by the sea, where you can happily count grains of sand.

Janno shook his head.

"No", he said, and spoke to the blue in the window, "no, Jirro. I don't want to. I simply don't want to anymore!"

He reached into the sink and let the screws flow between his fingers, a clean, shiny, dwindling stream. Janno pushed his cupped hands closer together, now the screws trickled, twinkling in the dim light, down onto the heap, gleaming arc, and as the trickling ebbed, Janno spoke quietly, startled by his own certainty: "We no longer understand each other, Jirro. It's as though, in the span of a single hour, I have made a leap into another existence: One can no longer continue in the same way one had wanted to, regardless of what happens afterwards. And I don't want to anymore, I don't want to anymore! I simply don't want to hear it any longer; "comrade causologist number 180, investigate why it is that this reacts in this manner-'; 'test this-'; 'research that-'; endlessly: that, that, that, on and on to some result that had been established before I even began, and never a "how", never a "whether", let alone a "what"."

And Janno, now beginning to understand that which had seemed completely incomprehensible, or rather: that which had seemed imaginable but never realistic (and thus all the more overwhelming), whispered it: "And then that assignment-" and he began—speaking at a normal volume again, though still as though he were delivering a monologue—what was special about that? Of course, his friend was right, of course a goal had been stipulated and needed to be reached. The predictions of the comrade classics had to be fulfilled, which, since analogous models were plentiful, could be done in a most reliable, if perhaps not especially intellectually challenging manner, with one of the proven deduction-induction-circles of absolute certainty about the exemplificandum -

and since it seemed to Janno as if Jirro's face had darkened, he quickly drew a concrete sketch of one of those circles: the comrades classics were always right when it came to problems of Greek sophism; the *sorites* paradox is a problem of Greek sophism; any problem of Greek sophism was a problem of the philosophy of the precursors to the comrade classic; any problem of philosophy of the precursors to the comrade classics was negated by the philosophy the comrade classics; the philosophy the comrade classics has achieved the status of a science; that which is superseded by science has reached its scientific solution; so the *sorites* paradox has also-

And Jirro finished: "reached its scientific solution."

Whereupon Janno quickly came to his conclusion, his example had interrupted. Indeed such circular reasoning would fulfill the requirements of the relevant assignment by demonstrating that the predictions of the comrade classics are fulfilled; yet—and now, hope to the wind, Janno's voice took on an unfamiliar quality—yet they had an opportunity of not just proving the prognosis, but actually fulfilling it. In other words, to solve the *sorites* paradox for real, not just rhetorically. And in this moment, confronting this alternative, a change came over Janno, driving him into the unknown, into unprescient depths, into the incalculable: "The problem, Jirro, at its purest, beyond any ulterior objective, in pure freedom –" and again he stated matter-of-factly: His friend would never understand.

Jirro's sad laughter: Everything had been reversed; Jirro's face now looked tortured, while Janno's face seemed almost peacefully relieved now that he had reached the other side of a difficult decision.

Was he witnessing a splitting of the moral core, a beta-ripple of the scientific conscience? The physicist examined the philosopher, how he stood there, stretched out in the streaks of light, luxury shoes and luxury watch, luxury perfume and fancy haircut, silver-gray tie matching his uniform, and now his vain laughter after that decision, silver-gray tie of thought; a singularity. One small push, thought Jirro, and everything will fall back into place, or was Janno going to pursue this further?

"This happens to everyone at some point in their life," he now said, as calm as Janno, "each of us must challenge the norm at some point, but you haven't learned how to renounce that desire yet. That's the next step, which you must take, since you can no longer stay as you are.

And now he started laughing too: "I'm further than you are."

No, said Janno, renouncing means going back.

Yes, said Jirro, it means going back, yet at the same time also reaching a higher level: we reserve the act of renunciation, as insight into the necessary, which we previously understood only in theory but not yet existentially. Imagine the movement of a spiral staircase—you circle back while moving up.

"Up where?" asked Janno.

Their looks converged on the heap, and suddenly the gleaming pile began to tremble, and simultaneously the window began to rattle; mud chips burst from the pane, and marching music boomed through the lab. At the same time, the siren began to wail, three times, long-short-long: institutional roll call.

Jirro was first to the window: "Our comrade captain of the capital monitoring troops is visiting!", and he held out his hand to his friend to say goodbye: they could work out the details of their deal later; Janno needed to go line up, get out of the lab; and Janno laughed: he wasn't lining up.

Trombones and bass drums.

Had he gone insane?

Not so—he was following the institutional rule which exempted urgent work from roll call; the assignment had been characterized as urgent, and there was truly nothing more urgent than his problem, and besides: he didn't want to anymore.

"How vain can you be?" said Jirro, "Stupid and vain! Do you have any idea what you're doing? First financing your own work, then independent thought? Man, get us all in trouble!"

He grabbed his friend by the shoulder: "I'm sorry, I was just worried about you!

The shawms blared; Jirro cried over them: "Your consciousness meter! Test yourself! This will be the ruin of you!"

Stomping and scrabbling could be heard through the droning sound of marching music. The philosophers lined up by department, in blocks: affirmators, causologists, syllologists, categorians, predicandists, apodictists, assertorians, light-footed young moralists in lock-step with the aestheticists, with their swarms of affiliated assistant thinkers, and - diligently aware of their responsibility of organizing the front—the second and first dialecticians with one and two silver bars on their work helmets, and now the higher ranks with golden stripes: chief Optimists, staff Optimists –

"Oh highest rational being, your leader is about to appear! Get out there!"

The march "We Cheerful Philosophers" rang out, the D-Major percussion of the united trumpets in octaves and fourths, overlaid in good spirits by French horn triplets, and through it all the stringency of the bass drum beat.

"For the last time, man: Get out there!"

Janno wasn't even shaking his head in protest anymore.—He turned to the camera, checked to make sure the film had been rolled further, threw a screw into the shoe box, took a photo, threw another screw; Jirro reached into the heap a second time.

A shrug of the shoulders: "Don't disturb my heap!"

The music stopped; numbers were called and marked present or absent. "Janno", said Jirro, "be reasonable, give me the twelve pounds. There's no doubt you'll end up in a research lab, and a deal's a deal.

Janno calmly counted out the money. Jirro gave him an imploring look.

"D-K 180!" rang across the parade grounds from the speakers, the voice of the causologist-in-chief (who held the rank of first dialectician), and Janno, passing the bills to Jirro, walked up to the window and smashed it.

"D-K 180's at work!" he called out.

A clatter of shards. Blood sprayed from the back of Janno's hand. Jirro rushed to the cupboard; of course, no first aid kit. Janno, raising his injured hand like a banner, walked to the sink, threw out a screw with his left hand, walked to the camera, pressed the release button (with his left hand), the lens shutter clicked, blood dripped, Jirro banged the cupboard shut, and from the speaker silence droned.

"It's still a heap, isn't it?" asked Janno.

Jirro dabbed his hand with a handkerchief.

From the speaker the voice of the causologist-in-chief: "Unbelievable dis-", and popping and silence; then sudden crackling, and the lock-step of a drilled battalion. "Jirro", Janno said to his friend, who was trying in vain to bind his friend's hand with a handkerchief that was much too short. "Jirro," he said it so calmly that the marching outside faded into a rushing sound, not unlike the one that blew across the grounds daily -: He had long wanted to ask him, the professional neutrinologist, what exactly it was, a neutrino—would he mind explaining it to him?

Holding his friend's hand in his own, closer than ever before, he saw a burning in his eyes that he had never seen before: Sure he could, Jirro assured him, now equally calm (what else could keep his friend calm) and through the shards of the window, a pure blue sky.

How many times had it been Jirro's job to answer these layman's questions, which made the unimaginable imaginable: during the open science weeks, for the monitoring troops, in schools; now, as he tore up the handkerchief and knotted the two strips together, he could hear the cheerful march across the parade grounds, quickly filling the chaos of silence with order, and it seemed to him as though he were answering this question for the first time. He listened with interest, yes, even astonishment, as though he were experiencing something unknown or better yet: as though something familiar had entered into a realm where it was never meant to go.

During the process of radioactive decay, or more precisely, during beta radiation, a highly unusual phenomenon emerges, which had posed a chilling challenge to science when it was first discovered: Even with the strictest measurements and monitoring, a considerable amount of energy disappears, despite the ultimate law of all existence which held that energy cannot disappear, which of course it wasn't doing: As research had shown in the previous century, it was actually captured by a particle which had no mass or charge, which essentially wasn't there at all, though obviously it had to exist, and was proven to exist, even if it couldn't fully be proven—

And so that, Janno interrupted him, is the neutrino, and Jirro corrected him: The neutrinos, since there are different kinds, divided into neutrinos and antineutrinos, and among them was one kind which was absolutely unprovable, because it definitely did not exist.

And now he had probably been given the task, Janno interrupted Jirro for the second time, with proving the existence of the impossible-to-prove particle, to thus prove the triumph of physics in a Truly Free Society—

How did he know that? Jirro wanted to ask, though Janno's deduction spoke for itself; the door slammed open and passing between two rows of monitoring troops, who immediately adopted a defensive stance, they entered: The captain of the capital monitoring troops and the philosopher-in-chief.

Janno, rather than identifying himself, asked in a friendly tone: "Can I help you?""; the philosopher-in-chief turned pale.

Jirro stepped forward.

"A workplace accident," he reported on his friend's behalf, and with irreproachable composure he provided Janno's identification number, according to regulation.

They beckoned him; he identified himself.

What was he doing here during work hours?

For some days now he had noticed that his friend, causologist 180, was increasingly starting to suffer from clouded consciousness –

That's not true! Janno sharply interrupted; unflinching, Jirro continued: that he was experiencing clouded consciousness, and since comrade DK 180, as far as he knew, was dealing with an especially urgent assignment –

How did he know that? Exposed, he remained silent; the comrade captain of the monitoring troops gave the comrade philosopher-in-chief a questioning look, what was this urgent assignment and what was the relevant security clearance level, yet before they could exchange inquiring looks, the causologist's thought leader (who held the rank of first dialectician) was on site and began explaining.

The philosopher-in-chief gave an ominous look, the captain a bright one.

Blood continued dripping from Janno's bound hand.

"What? Asked the captain of the monitoring troops, his animated tone butting through the gloomy silence, "a heap, what's it called: *sororities*? And that's what the costly materials were for?

Whistling through his teeth: real screws; he let them flow between his fingers; the captain of the monitoring troops shook their heads with rehearsed timing, flashing their helmet, they all seemed appalled: True metal screws in a trash can, oh atoms, it was unfathomable!

This explains the shortage of screws in the production offices, the captain of the monitoring troops almost cheerfully stated, this would certainly interest their comrades in production, that's the weekly product of three crews, going to waste there in the sink of their comrade the intellectual. Looking at the philosopher-in-chief, whose face was rapidly darkening, and whose intensity, in contrast to the brightness of his counterpart, was rapidly escalating to the level of a challenge, his eyes were no longer questioning.

Jirro, who was no longer of importance to them, had time to look him over, the way he was standing there: without his protective helmet, in black uniform pants, his corpulence, his fat rolled up like his sleeves, self-confident in his shiny boots, and though neatly ordered, his jowls and the furrow between his brows revealed a deeply embedded tendency to brood, awakened by instinct, strengthened by experience, and already weighing, out of self-interest, the efficacy of how the others had handled the situation, and the degree of their guilt in order to determine how he could carry out their punishment.

Jirro saw, almost with a sense of admiration, how this kind of thinking turned to action: An unnoticeable deepening of a crease through the raising of the eyelids over both focused pupils; quietly sucking in air; a fleeting twitch of the chin, and the disapproval of his troops was perfectly frozen in the look he was giving the philosopher-in-chief, to whom all eyes had turned, including Janno's.

The philosopher-in-chief, fat like his counterpart, albeit less in the manner of a jovial boxer than a butcher in need of protection, suddenly darkened so quickly that all eyes followed his to his subordinate, with the question of whether someone could finally explain to him what the meaning was of this monstrous squandering of materials for this—what was it called? *Socrates*?—anyway, for this crap, and the causologist thought leader, also fat, short of stature, slick and brisk, who passed on the question without hesitation to his subordinate through a single look, and then a single raised finger, at last in little bursts of rage. Film, for example, he cried out, what's with that, he had never ordered that, they should show him the records, immediately, on the spot—

and all stared at the device, how it stood there, black, cowered in silence, its giant eye trained on the sink, in which the screws bloomed in pure innocence, and Jirro froze: If Janno were to reveal that he's been funding this himself! He could already see himself paying for all of the equipment, just so he could spend even more years using it *not* to prove the unprovable neutrino; and there, in the face of this looming catastrophe, yet entirely ignorant of the other danger, namely that his sudden move could put his life at risk, he pulled out the consciousness meter and pressed it to Janno's head.

As the probe penetrated his brain, automatically extended by the device, the three leaders, who were now standing around them, the indication pointer steadily quivered around the maximum point of the most extreme consciousness clouding, which, pending an exact diagnosis by the computer inside the device, prescribed the imminent and urgent evacuation of the test subject to the nearest sanitarium.

Jirro saw it too; his only thought: had the danger been averted? Pushed back by his corpulent comrades, he glanced at Janno; the probe had made him smile with soothing music, which placated the will, relaxed the muscles, and stimulated linear thinking, and since Janno, as the melodic rhythms inaudibly dispersed, stood facing the camera, he thought that they were taking a group portrait. He smiled.

"There you see it," said their comrade the causologist thought leader, eagerly scanning the conscientiogram, which the machine now spat out as the probe retracted. "It's clear, he's sick-" and the philosopher-in-chief, face still darkened, asked: Sick? How could you give one of the most urgent assignments that the philosophical institute has ever faced to someone with impaired consciousness? Despite having only recently arrived in this post, he had immediately realized with horror what a heap of vermin he was dealing with here (and Jirro admiringly recognized the twofold strategy behind this assessment: protection and counterstrike in one), here, like everywhere, this vermin had managed to seize the upper hand, but he would crush this heap with an iron fist -

There the captain of the monitoring troops quickly interrupted him (while the causologist thought leader did the only thing he could think of in this battle of leadership: slip back towards the door, smiling, though he didn't get past the sink) and, crumpling the conscientogram like a handkerchief into the pocket of his pants while pensively staring at the forethinker, he cut off their maneuvers by offering an olive branch: "It has been shown, time and again, that no matter how big a dangerous heap of internal enemies there is, their number is in rapid decline", a final remnant of the eternally unfree who had survived the long conquered past, but who could now comfortably be counted on two hands! Here he spread his hands, each finger a gallows for one of the few, and with this bold gesture, his voice took on an admonitory seriousness: In light of such enlightening words, the most difficult questions became clear, as well as the undoubtedly highly complicated problems of their comrade philosopher for whose commendable work he of course had the highest admiration.

Benevolently, he looked around the room. Each person moved by their own motivations, now united in nodding: Jirro looked overwhelmed; the forethinker officious, the philosopher-in-chief emerged from his dark mood; so around the circle, slowly gradually. They moved in time with the men from the monitoring troops, their perpendicular shiny helmets with their flaming sword of affirmation, two of whom now approached Janno, who waited for them as though in a dream, immersed in the bliss of the self-fulfilling thought that reality seemed to shape itself around him.

And as Jirro, in a sudden rush of insight, grasped the solution to the *sorites* paradox, he called out, as though he were guessing Janno's thoughts, to the captain of the monitoring troops: "Smile!" and ran to the camera and captured them in his frame: The philosopher-in-chief, not quite quick enough to dodge the camera, the causologist thought leader all the way in the back, causologist 180 with his comrades from the monitoring troops who had their arms around him, and—a flower for the souvenir photo—in the laboratory sink the heap of screws.

While the captain of the monitoring troops was already formulating potential titles for this document in his mind ("*Incredible Squandering of Production Assets in the Institute of Philosophy Uncovered*") and the philosopher-in-chief, the same title in mind, stretched out his hand in acquiescence and thanked him on behalf of the institute for his inspiring words, Jirro shot like a star to the *sorites* paradox. A heap—or more precisely: the quantity of its quality, was always exactly that which was to be regarded as a heap in the interest of the Truly Liberated Society, in this case, using the heap of internal parasites as an example: a giant amount yet only a few.

In the steely light of this insight, the captain of the monitoring troops grabbed the right hand of the philosopher-in-chief, gripping their hands with his left as well and warmly shaking on it, while outside the court of philosophers launched into a newly intoned version of the Song of Absolute Certainty. There: in the happiness of solved philosophemes, and simultaneously in the suddenly growing sense of aching sadness that Janno would never have a chance to celebrate this solution (since it went without saying that his treatment would commence with the erasure of all memory from at the least the most recent years, Janno came to another realization. In the mix of joy and sorrow, which were competing with one another to the point of exhaustion, he recognized the most pressing problem of this difficult day: smuggling his heap of ten screws out of the institute of philosophy, past the magnet straps of the monitoring troops, which detected the tiniest amounts of metal.

Crushed by the irrefutable necessity of making a decision, his realization became a different form of pacifying music, in that it completely paralyzed Jirro's decision-making ability. Meanwhile, in the dissolution of the handshake between the comrades, the monitoring troops were already getting back into formation, keeping an eye on Jirro while looking to their leader for orders. The latter, however, was busy calculating whether it would be smart to take on the Physics Trust. At this point, Jirro had become utterly incapable of making a simple but urgent inquiry as to whether he, neutrinologist 476, might return to work (let alone asking them to whom he should address this inquiry).

In this moment everything that was undecided (since even the philosopher-in-chief was reconsidering, weighing whether he could shift blame to this intruder, the consequences of endangering his relationship with the physics board, over which he might have to preside as early as the following morning), so in this dark, problematic moment, where all thought faltered at a crossroads, forcing the expressions and postures of everyone present into unfathomable stoicism-: in this moment of pure introspection, Janno's thoughts pushed their way out with determination, moving to the rhythm of the pacifying music: Face wide open, he looked at the captain of the monitoring troops, and said, in the innocence of his absolute certainty: "But he's not in the picture!"

And while, outside, the cheerful philosophers praised, in the refrain of their guild song, the testing of all theory in practice, Janno tried to wrest one arm from the troops' embrace, to bring back the person who was missing from the group portrait.

A pure misunderstanding of word and movement: his smile cracked, his goodwill broke, an artery throbbed in his brow fat, a roar broke out, and then it was over; and "It's over! It's over!" the philosopher-in-chief cried out, to the truly guilty party in this scandal, searching for the causologist thought leader. It's over, thought the monitoring troops. It's over! thought Jirro too, and then, in one fell swoop, Janno broke free and approached the man he'd been thinking about, and as Janno got closer, the man's face turned white as chalk, his cry turned to grimace, his eyes filled with raw, naked fear; he raised his hands to cover his eyes, which, unconcealed mirrors of the soul, had widened with a deadly fear. Coming at him were his deepest fears turned flesh in the form of his assassin, and the philosopher-in-chief saw his shock and recognized in him the fear of his enemy, and as he now knew this weakness, a sense of victory blazed in his eyes. The monitoring troops, clenched their fists around the steel of their beta-brownings, whipped from their shoulder holsters, and Jirro recognized in them the glow of certainty that nobody would be paying any attention to the magnet straps nor would they stop his self-removal, and in that moment of pure revelation, a light appeared in Janno's eyes as well, the bliss of insight.

We cannot know what revealed itself to him, as he was looking at the group portrait, the heap of all his beloved Comrades. Perhaps he saw solution to the *sorites* paradox, or perhaps just the sun in its freedom, maybe the grime on the shards of the window pane, framed by the colours of the rainbow, but we no longer know that.

Monument

If Jirro, the certified neutrinologist, had been asked—which he was not –what essential insight he had gained from being one of those permitted, through of an exchange program, to work for seventy weeks in Libroterr, in the other half of the world, he would have answered: a better understanding of his own country. Now, he probably would have actually said something different, but we know of at least one instance in which the strange land of Libroterr so illuminated the essential structure of his own society, like lightning before his eyes and mind, that he was overwhelmed by it and wrote in his diary that if there were to be a monument to his native Uniterr, it would have to be the mountain factory of Moritz Cornelius Asher.

Jirro's diary entry, written as it is in the conditional, is shamefully imprecise for a scientist, especially a certified neutrinologist: Uniterr has in fact erected plenty of monuments to Uniterr. Jirro ought to have formulated it like this: if an architectural or physical structure is so capable of expressing the essence of a society that it could serve as a monument to it, then this factory is it for Uniterr. No doubt about it. The factory of M.C. Asher was built during Jirro's research exchange, and the fact that Jirro witnessed the whole process, from its beginning as mere whispers, through its construction, all the way to its final product, was what drove him to write in such terms.

The factory, a blinding-white structure—in colour and compactness resembling certain fortresses in Uniterr—rested there on a stone outcropping on the mountain face, on a silicum ledge above the tree line but below the icy heights. It had such an awkward shape that there was space for only two openings to the outside world: the pipe through which the pure mountain spring water flowed, and the gate where the workers streamed in and out. It did not take much imagination to see in this passage, which was so difficult to traverse, a symbol for a country whose borders could only be crossed by a select few. Jirro saw the gate as the point at which the generations gave way to one another: birth and death, may it always be so. The rest of it was sheer, bare, blinding-white walls; no windows, no entrances; no chimney, no drainage. Whatever may have been rumbling deep inside, not a sound could be heard from the outside. It stood there looming like destiny over the rooftops: silent and monstrously eternal.

No one could imagine that it was not as old as the mountains themselves.

The factory was one of a kind: it did not, properly speaking, produce anything, or if it did, then its product was a new kind of physics, or rather the material substrate of one. It served, as Jirro put it, to produce new laws of physics that could never have occurred naturally. It was sort of as if one were to apply the taxonomies of the various species of moss to the class of mammals and call it a new kind of botany. It would be necessary to create whole new kinds of mammals. No, there is no reasonable analogy for it: there is a factory, and it does produce something. Its creator, Moritz Cornelius Asher, the only son of the legendary M. C. Asher I, the arcade king of Libroterr, was fascinated from a young age by his discovery that the magical collision of the coloured steel and ivory balls in his father's pinball-world could be calculated. Already as a child he became obsessed with mechanics. Instead of reading and writing, he studied the laws of incidence and reflection. He was not interested in any game that he could not calculate, for indeed he enjoyed the calculating more than the playing. He stayed true to his childhood passion and followed the advice of the pinball management and his teachers by studying ten years of physics. By now the owner of a particle accelerator and going by the name M.C. II, he had worked his way into the microcosmos of matter. When he discovered the laws of that domain, he was at first shocked, then horrified, and he took it upon himself to change that world.

What horrified him was the impossibility of making exact calculations of the location and momentum of a single particle, ruling out any chance of encountering in the microcosm his beloved laws of mechanics. He wouldn't accept it. They told him about a law of nature that ruled out such an exact knowledge, a certain "Heisenberg uncertainty principle," which only hardened his refusal to accept such sloppiness. Who made the laws anyway: man or nature? And even if it had been nature so far, did it have to stay that way forever? Or everywhere? Even in the innermost essence of all materials, in the innermost core of an atom? Even there—so said M.C. II, relying more on his unbending will than on sound deductions—even in the chaotic behavior of the elementary building blocks (what had once been known as "pudding," the particles finally recognized as underlying quarks) it must be within the power of human creativity to bring the confused swarm of the most miniscule bodies into the tidy order of mechanical relationships.

"Who makes the laws: man or the pudding?" he repeated at his next lecture, and threw pudding powder at the professor, after which his classmates starting calling him "Professor Pudding." The rector filed a complaint; M.C. I shook his head thoughtfully. Mechanics in the microcosmos, that offered completely new possibilities: an electron microscope in every home, and little games of pinball on the microscope slide: neutron races, electron fencing, meson billiards, proton poker, and all this inside the crystal lattice of the atoms. A whole new market was opening up! He took his son out of the university and told him to develop his theory; M.C II did just that, calling his theory "micromechanics." Its sheer simplicity trumped every attempt to disprove it—for all ingenious ideas are simple. In the microcosmos, the principles of mechanics are present, if not, admittedly, actively, then at least latently, as a kind of possibility—how else could they have the effects that they undeniably have in the macrocosmos? So it was only a matter of transforming the latency into activity, which had to be possible by applying some ordering force that had not yet been discovered. He could apply pressure with a chamber of appropriate dimensions, and the necessary degree of compactness could be calculated. What can be calculated can be constructed. What can be constructed can be realized. Ergo: micromechanics is proven.

This was ingenious in its simplicity, and M.C. I rubbed his hands in delight. But now, for reasons that were never made clear, things took a fateful turn: M.C. II became a moralist. Just as he had made atomic physics subordinate to micromechanics, he now made micromechanics subordinate to ethics, spoiling any hope of marketing it. Jirro tried to make sense of this development as a result of M.C. II's ongoing disappointment at the disappearance of his beloved mechanics; psychologists spoke of a delayed and therefore particularly intense suppression of the anal-sadistic phase of development. Their explanation had a lot in common with Jirro's and was based primarily on the frequent use of words with a moral connotation, words like "pure," "slag," and "purge" in his treatises on micromechanics, or, to be more precise, in its ethical programming. Others had yet other explanations for it; but these were never fully satisfying, especially not for the pinball-king as he watched all his son's promising theories lose themselves in abstruseness. Or perhaps "abstruse" is not the right word, for when M.C. II published tracts—anyone in Libroterr was allowed to publish—he claimed to have given micromechanics to the world in order "to reform the materials of base nature in fulfillment of their potential," "to bring them into line with pure being," or "to endow them with their own possibilities," or even "to elevate nature to a higher level," and all the typical enthusiastic ravings of a moralist, or to put it more openly: of a maniac. His father hired the best psychiatrists; they followed all the traditional prescriptions. They asked the patient about his dreams, only to be told that he did not dream. He was not lying: his powers of imagination were devoted entirely to his waking life, excessive thought-games about a reconfiguration of the earth through the reconfiguration of the elements into their micromechanically ordered forms, which he would manufacture one after the other: ordered helium, ordered hydrogen, ordered lithium, and so on all the way to ordered bicinicum (atomic number 169).

To create the world anew, and thus elevate it to its true being—that was what M.C. II thought of in his dreams and dreamed about in his thoughts, and when his dreams carried him out of the smoky city to the fields and the mountains, he broke out of the structures of methodological schemes and dreamed in sensual concreteness: water from the glacial spring—he was convinced that this had to be his starting material. A baptism of mind and fantasy, and suddenly, in a vision of a new dawn, he saw micromechanically ordered water in its concrete otherness: water in absolute purity. A water that had never existed before; he looked upon it with ecstasy. Until then the impure version of water had had to suffice, and just as he had come to understand the shape of spheres in his childhood, he began to grasp the form of water; he wandered along the mountain streams towards their source, ran naked through the rain, gathered snowflakes and clouds, and the water thanked him for it: once, a drop of dew resting on an oak leaf showed him in the magnified pattern of veins the blueprint of the great transformation machine he would build; another time, in the inverted image of the world reflected in a puddle, he saw the forms of the hanging flues, that ingenious principle of augmented gravity, which offered a surplus of energy, which he then applied to the whole system. He also began reading up on water, and soon he came across Thales, and his theory of water as the origin of all being gave him the philosophical support he needed to remain firm in his conviction and resist the armies of psychiatrists that M.C. I inexhaustibly called up against him. He won a few of them over; they were the founders of psychohomeopathy.

And so in the face of all resistance, M.C. II had the plans for his factory in his head, and soon it was committed to paper and secure in a platinum safe (a present from the board for his twelfth birthday), when

(an explosion during the attempt to build an electron pool table after all; it was generally believed that it was an act of revenge by his son, even though all the signs pointed to his business rivals)

his father died at so opportune a time, before he could disinherit the moralist, who now as the sole heir to an unimaginable fortune, in the prime of his life, was in a position to make his dream a reality. It made no difference that the project was insanity, as there were no legal obstacles in his way; the site, the mountain land, was a part of his inheritance, and Libroterr has no other regulations. The contractors leapt at the job; it was a chance to test new techniques with no risk. As the structure grew, so did the rumors, and since the man behind it all remained persistently silent, the press had their sensation: "*New factory to turn water into oil?*" asked Libroterr's largest newspaper. "*A gambling den under the mountain??*" asked its competitor.

Jirro was there for the groundbreaking, and he will never forget that the first stone laid was itself a "pudding," that it was an act of pure thought that contained the force of eight hydrogen bombs in this pudding as it sank into the bedrock, so that no one present noticed a thing.

Even for Libroterr, the project was grandiose: the overload pressure chamber alone (which was necessary to turn micromechanical energy, if there turned out to be any such thing, into actual energy) had to withstand a force strong enough to move the whole mountain, and so was two kilometers in diameter, but still had a capacity of less than half a liter. The flues stretched two hundred meters into a cleft ten times as large; the transformation machine itself was a pure-gold Möbius strip, through which the raw material poured down into the chamber, and, having been micromechanically ordered, drawn up out of it again; the gear in its heart was a diamond the size of a child's head. But the most intricate part of the structure was the apparatus for cleaning the raw materials: a system of grates and filters stacked obliquely to the rock face and glaciers, which secured against biological, chemical, and physical contamination, and under that—that is, in the middle of the vault—a sieve made of anti-matter, of anti-water, to be precise, which, although it could not touch the water, served as catalyst for the transformation from latency to potency. The creator considered it invaluable.

A miracle of human willpower, it took sixty weeks to build, longer than an artificial sun. Every day during those sixty weeks offered so many feasts for the eye that, since there was nothing covering the construction site, Jirro had to decide every morning between the actual purpose of his exchange (the observation of a certain practically unobservable neutrino, which theoretically did not exist) and the urge to go and admire the construction. Where in Uniterr were stone sanders that fit into your pocket like flashlights? What about lunar reflectors? And viscous gas for safety in transport?

Even Libroterr was amazed; so many people came to gape at the construction that the trains to the site had to be closed to the public during shift changes. The tourist agencies set up parallel tracks, and of course *flotels*—flying hotels—as well; too expensive for Jirro's stipend.

But the most amazing thing was that the excitement went on unabated for five quarters (enough time for the pharma-trends to shift seven times): even when the dedication day came, no one knew precisely what product to expect from the factory, only that thanks to something called micromechanics, which was laughed at by the experts, water was supposed to undergo some kind of transformation—but how and into what, no one had any idea. M.C. II kept talking about a new natural order, about how the elements would self-actualize into the highest forms of their own being, but what that meant concretely, he did not care to explain. And so the rumors, fed by the press, spiraled out of control; an enterprising lottery acquired the worldwide monopoly on betting markets for what the final product would be; a sect of "micromechanical sophists" popped up, in order to form an opposition right away; in certain theological circles they lamented mankind's retreat into superstitions long since abandoned, in certain mathematical circles they spoke of a new miracle at Cana.

Jirro did not understand these allusions, and he was too embarrassed to ask. Shortly before the opening, his proposal to test M.C. Asher's theories mathematically and develop a computer model to simulate micromechanics, to finally determine whether this project had any value, was met with a regretful shake of the head: was there a contract from industry for it? Well, then.

Such lessons left Jirro helpless: Libroterr with all its contradictions, not least between its monstrosity and its provincialism, became ever more incomprehensible to him. He could not find the rules by which to orient himself, and when he met with irony where he had expected agreement, and once more recognized that his and his colleagues' thoughts were running obliquely without ever intersecting, he longed for straightforward Uniterr. Everything there was so well-ordered, so comprehensible, so predictable!

What completely baffled Jirro was the role of industry in this society, which faced no obstacles in creating for itself insane projects, indeed ones that required madmen (Libroterr's newspapers praised M.C. II as "the savior of business," while the union press even suggested erecting a monument to him while he was still alive, and 872 unemployed sculptors immediately sent in proposals) and so set its sights on efforts simply overwhelming in comparison to Uniterr's humbler ambitions. There were flying hotels, for instance, that could be built in eight hours; and everyone was amazed that Jirro was amazed at them. Jirro became bitter; he was ashamed of his country, and once, when he discovered how comfortable the train to the factory was (at first he had not dared to take the trains, which he had assumed, because of their adjustable seat-cushions, were only for high-ranking officials), he was so taken with shame that he hit a colleague in the face over a joke about Uniterr's streets, which won him praise from the newly-appointed attaché for micromechanics at the Uniterran embassy. "Heroic action in defense of our beloved fatherland!" and: "egregious agitation on the part of the enemy resisted!" and: "our scientists put to the test!"—Such were the headlines in Uniterr's newspaper honoring the incident. They published letters from readers, who overwhelmingly expressed their pride at being citizens of a country that had produced neutrinologists like Jirro. The attaché for micromechanics composed a report to the government in which he ascribed Jirro's patriotic zeal to his, the attaché's, educational influence; he was promoted to senior attaché. The fact that he had held his office for only three days at the time of the event was not taken into consideration; when Jirro heard about the promotion, he discovered a new talent for cynicism.

At the gala opening of the factory (admission tickets in the form of penny stock were traded at exorbitant prices) the senior attaché for micromechanics was personally invited by M.C. Asher, along with his twelve-man delegation; the diplomat also requested Jirro's company. When, climbing out of the train, the citizens of Uniterr caught sight of the work under the glacier, without any banners or flags, even on dedication day, without any festoons, without even a wreath to draw the eye, only a white building on the silver silicon ledge, and not even a bit of smoke, the senior attaché remarked that this was, veritably, a true instantiation of Libroterr's misanthropic character and proof that Uniterr had surpassed it historically. He did not say why, and everyone nodded.

"The dying half of the world," said the diplomat. That hits the nail on the head, Jirro confirmed. Then the gate slammed shut behind him.

The production, still shrouded in mystery (the top bets for what the final product would be stood as follows: 3-2 for natural gas, 2-1 for gold, 5-1 for plutonium, 18-1 for artificial blood, 18.5-1 for natural manure; bearish bets on no product at all were not accepted), began with an address from M.C. II.

He stood, dressed entirely in black, a radiant brimmed hat on his head, on a pure platinum podium.

He knew, so he began thoughtfully—speaking like a man who had learned to be silent and allow his thoughts to ripen—he knew how eagerly mankind, including those on the other side of the bor-

(and here he improvised a small bow to the representatives of Uniterr, who, responded in unison with broad, bashful smiles)

-der, had been awaiting this moment, the moment of the triumph of micromechanics, which was called upon to lead the wasteland of nature at last through a process of purification to its proper calling. And he knew also, he said after a pause, during which he cast his gaze, as did the guests, around the hall, the interior of which matched the exterior. Rows of blinding white blocks and cubes, all covered, no machines in sight, invisible too were the condensation chambers and the hanging flues, no windows, no gates, and the whole interior was bathed in shadowless light; even the transformation machine was hidden, but its cover was so transparent that the diamond gear remained visible through the gold of the Möbius strip. He knew also that certain circles (and then the voices rose up into a murmur of indignation, which he seemed to enjoy) had called him a madman, some even called him a charlatan, who dreamed up a project with no intention of bringing it to fruition, which is why he (and here he raised his hand to quiet the rising indignant murmurs), had come up with a perfect way to silence all these voices: he had here (he pounded lightly on his podium), here in a safe a precise prediction of what would now, through micromechanics, happen to the wa-

(he turned on a spotlight, the light of which, piercing the walls of the factory and the mountain's rock face, showed the spring deep inside the granite, which now, guided by the will of man, came pouring through all the sieves and grates as far as the feeder gate in front of the Möbius strip)

-ter, what's more to the pure water, or, to be more precise: the glacial water considered until now to be pure, what would be done to this water through elemental ordering.

And when he opened the feeder gate (and once again through a mental act) a second spotlight shone into the depths of the mountain factory, in which –

while in the glowing green plasma the absolute darkness of the anti-water began to boil—the water in the chamber began to seethe and foam; and while the visitors were overwhelmed with the sight of the purple smoke cascading down the hanging flues, heightening the condensation pressure to the necessary degree by the force of its fall, Jirro saw the creator of all this gazing with a look of ecstasy into the tumbling water, as if he saw with some inner eye the ordering power at work, the power now beginning to bring into alignment the atoms in the molecules, the ions in the atoms, the quarks in the ions, the pudding in the quarks: a game of pool with subatomic particles, calculable even unto the most distant future.

And M.C. II *beheld* the order, pure in its complete purity, and, unfolding a piece of parchment that slid out of the podium towards him, he announced that—it was witnessed by a notary—this text, written sixty weeks ago, contained the precise prediction of what would happen to the water from the glacial spring from the time when it entered the transformation machines until it left; and

(meanwhile the description of the ongoing process was projected onto the walls—including the colour of the smoke in the hanging flues, which the visitors had seen and continued to see)

while the newly-ordered water slowly, surely, blessedly, proudly climbed back up the Möbius strip, he stepped, his head framed by the glowing brim of his hat, which, as if all the light in the hall were drawn to the creator, began imperiously to shine on the man who had dreamed up this work, towards a basin on the lower end of the transformation works, in which the water was slowly approaching a transparent pipe, and opening with his own hands a tap at the bottom of the basin, Moritz Cornelius Asher II spoke the following words, and at the same moment they appeared in burning black letters on the wall:

THERE SHALL BE ORDER!

THERE SHALL BE PURITY!

THE TRUE ERA OF THE COSMOS IS BEGINNING!

And while the final product began to collect at the bottom of the basin and the boiling in the ordering chamber rumbled on like the droning of an organ, he declared from within a glistening, radiant circle, one hand raised up while the other pointed into the basin, with the clear voice of the self-evident, that micromechanics had succeeded, without the slightest outside help, through nothing but the material's own self-order, to refine the water that had always been considered pure, to actual, absolute purity, to the most unique essence of its own being: free—

(and in the basin there arose, swelling up in waves, emitting a penetrating musty stench, a grey, slimy brew)

free from any external power, free to be absolutely unworkable for any human pleasure or purpose.

The Street of Perversions

When Jirro, the certified neutrinologist, was given the enviable privilege of leaving his native Uniterr and spending seventy weeks in Libroterr as part of a scientific exchange program, he used to enjoy taking long walks after the working day. Whatever city he was in, he would walk in the alleys behind the buildings whose fronts overlooked the grand thoroughfares, like the so-called Great Ring of the capital city. Not only to avoid being bothered by predator ads (these were unheard of in Uniterr, but in Libroterr they were a common way of catching a mark, in which a startling optical sensation, say, a hologram of a living horse, grabs the victims' attention and they—usually tourists—are then asked whether they liked what they saw, and if they say yes, a fee is demanded, or even taken by force, since there's no law against it and, besides, the victim doesn't want any trouble, and so usually pays without a fuss; the trick is just to ignore the ads, or say no).

But it wasn't just because of predator ads and the like (the main streets were teeming with hustlers) that Jirro didn't walk beneath the front facades of Libroterr's buildings: he was after something else. And that something was a sound-show that fascinated him and piqued his imagination like nothing else, without costing a thing: the tapestry of sounds from Libroterr's televisions. The usual spot for a television receiver is in the living room, and hardly anyone, at least in Libroterr, lives in an apartment overlooking the main streets. Those are reserved for technical equipment: elevators, moving hallways, toilets, pneumatic delivery tubes and garbage chutes, physio-climate-control and psycho-climate-control, and the entrances for the helicopter taxis, which can be quite messy as they whir in and out. It can be dangerous to show yourself at the front window; all the parades, bank robberies, kidnappings, sports competitions, and everything else worth seeing is much more clearly and conveniently accessible from the closed circuit stations. And so most people live in the quiet back apartments, and the television sets are found back where people live, and since they aren't turned off even at night, and since—Jirro could not overcome his amazement—there were tens of thousands of channels in Libroterr compared to just one in Uniterr (there had once been three hours a week devoted to the local stations classified by Uniterr's statistical survey as "independent," but even those nine stations, Liechtenstein, Schliersee I and II, Vatican,

Nanjing, "Voice of the Antarctic," Nagyszentbalatonhúzenketökisvasarhelyifüröd, Uganda, and Giza, were all merged together, starting in the great year of unification, 2001, and eventually—Schliersee I was the last, holding out until 2054—came to constitute the single unified broadcaster "Free Uniterr") yes, since there were so many channels in Libroterr, and since they were all available everywhere (everywhere in Libroterr, that is) walking by the open windows one could hear, if not every program, at least as many programs as there were residents in that particular building, and sometimes a few more.

Now Jirro could have watched television at home (and he did often enough) or in any club, and if he had, he would have been able to choose what program to watch. But that wasn't the point. His tapestry of sounds was more than television, even if it seems like miss something by only listening to something meant to be watched. But the constraint was just what excited Jirro: to complement the words and the music with his imagination; and like a bolt of lightning the recognition hit him, that here, in this chasm between the buildings, hidden from the sky, the soul of the city opened itself to him, yes, even the soul of all of Libroterr, of half of the world.

Since that time he had taken to calling these back alleys his "streets of revelation."

The content of Libroterr's television was so different from Uniterr's that Jirro misunderstood a great deal at first. He can still recall his shock when once, taking refuge from a predator ad, he ducked behind one of the apartment buildings on the Great Ring and heard soft music through the open window, and then a cry of, *not in the kidneys!* followed by the clinking of steel and a devilish laughter. It is a testament to Jirro's character that he overcame his fear and dashed into the house to help; the fact, which soon came to light, that this scream was part of a popular science program for children—basic anatomy taught through a detective story—does nothing to lessen Jirro's courage. The scream, the music, the devilish laughter, it all turned out to be nothing: this was the street of revelation. From that moment on, Jirro was hooked. At first he reveled in the sheer variety, indulging first in its excess (once he listened to thirty-five programs at once) then in the number of variations on the two basic structures which he believed he recognized recurring again and again. Soon he was proud to have a formula for them: the violence of desire, and the desire for violence. All the music and all the dialogue come down to this. Finally he became captivated with the baffling texture of details woven by pure chance as he walked from window to window, from floor to floor. Jirro was enough of a scientist to retain these combinations in order to systematically analyze them (was there something like mesons and neutrinos in the realm of moral thinking?). Even though he destroyed his diaries and tapes before returning to Uniterr, what he heard had such an effect on him, and his zeal for analysis was so strong, that even years after returning home he could reconstruct these combinations in his head.

The first aural scene that Jirro created, even if it was rather subtle and not especially conspicuous, began as the intersection of a round of applause from a higher window with snatches coming from a lower window of someone running and—the sound of running suddenly broke off, but the applause kept going, kept on cheering at a silence made ghastly given what came before. The sound had been of someone running in fear: the sound of two bare feet fleeing down a dully-echoing corridor, and it didn't end with a lucky escape, since there would have been some sound to indicate as much, and it was not a scene change on the screen that Jirro could not see, since the background music, undertones of horror and death, continued unchanged. Yes, the fugitive was trapped. And the applauding crowd one level up, along with the music that coursed through all of Uniterr and Libroterr so constantly that only when it stopped did anyone think of it, was the pursuer coming inexorably closer. Now there were shouts of "bravo!" and pounding feet, shrill whistles of delight. Jirro stood stock still, following the course of the silence and wondering if he dared ask where those feet had fled to, or if they had been saved after all (for they had subconsciously awoken the memory of a nightmare):

While Jirro stood considering whether to knock on the apartment door, a storm broke out one floor up, the rumble of stormclouds, the whipping of the tree tops, and, below, a fist pounding on steel, resonating mutedly down the corridor, and over the surface of a round of applause the menacing steps come closer; the applause breaks off; now only the sweep of the sky which grows ever more unbearable and must resolve into a scream, and the sounds of a seductive crooning voice: *climb into my dreamboat, climb in, climb in.*

What came next, now dissolving into its individual parts, didn't quite come together: another love song, an ad for air spray, a conversation about doors and dogs, yet another song and then some more words and some thunder or something—Jirro soon learned that all the constellations that fascinated him did so by creating the illusion of a unity of action, an illusion which could not last long. This one had already lasted a comparatively long time. The next combination was appreciably shorter: the crashing of waves, foaming up over the breakers, and from the window opposite the moaning of two lovers coupling in perfect rhythm with the rolling sea, and suddenly a bellowing fog horn. Humorous consonances of this sort were rare; the most common, the ones that came up every day and constituted the vast majority, were the juxtaposition and superimposing of the two basic themes: the sounds of torture set to the crooning of a love song, the same structure as that first sound tapestry.

Jirro was so caught up in looking for such patterns that he missed the changes inside himself brought about by life in Libroterr. It was not long (Jirro never realized how short a time it was) before the crass obscenities, the crass brutalities, the crass monstrosities that were everywhere in Libroterr, and which had troubled him so much at first, came to seem normal. He grew so accustomed to them that he forgot how things had been in Uniterr, as though forgetting a dream after waking, or like an adult forgetting his earliest childhood. Out of sight, out of mind—isn't that what they say? That was part of it, but he had other things on his mind. The fading of his memories of Uniterr was accompanied by the rising feeling that he had crossed over from some imaginary realm into true reality. Granted, it was just a feeling, not his considered opinion. Jirro did not think about how Libroterr had come to seem normal to him and Uniterr only some sort of shadow. He had only a vague sense that something was amiss, as when he caught himself laughing at something that once would have struck him as grotesque and monstrous. Then he was ashamed; something inside of him protested strongly.

Jirro's conscience did catch up with him once. He was walking along behind the buildings of the Great

Ring, perhaps on his way to some rendezvous, and in a hurry. He was only listening with one ear, as usual, when a sudden sound made him start. It was a sinister, penetrating sizzle, like when a leaking psycho-climate-control unit emits the highly pressurized, highly toxic gas hypocyan amyl nitrate, and if he hadn't also heard the standard dialogue, a victim begging his captor to painlessly vaporize her instead of forcing her to suffer a horrible death by asphyxiation, Jirro would have thought something horrible was really happening. It was only a crime movie (the 328th entry of the relatively obscure series "It Could Happen To You Tonight"), and Jirro inadvertently shortened his stride. Torturing someone to death with gas, that was a new one, but nevertheless he could picture every detail perfectly. It helped that the killer was scornfully narrating it all to his victim, who appeared to be in a glass cage so that he could see the gas at work. There's no need to give the details: it was a minutely detailed description of a face turning white and a ribcage seized with convulsions, of the lungs inside it sucking in their own demise all the more eagerly the more it ravages them. This must have been a real feast for the eyes, and Jirro, even as he listened with a mixture of horror, enchantment, and nausea, stayed where he was and watched the scene with his ears, and imagined the victim as a woman, even though there was no reason to; he heard the murderer's whispers, and imagined two discoloured lips, when—

Suddenly the abrupt, shrill sound of a bicycle bell woke Jirro from his reverie. He jumped in guilty fear that an informer for Uniterr's feeling police might be watching him from behind one of the windows. He took off, and noticed as he was running away (an automatic selector set to your wishes or even better to your appetites can flip through all the channels almost instantly) the ecstatic outline of a gaping mouth coming from every window. As Jirro ran through the illuminated gulley between the buildings, he grew agitated and ashamed at having fallen prey to such reprehensible stuff—it all seemed repulsive to him now. Even as he was running away, he told himself that his interest was only scientific and systematic.

He was unable to do anything for the rest of the day.

In the lab the next day, under some mysterious urge to tell his Libroterran colleague what had happened, Jirro was uncharacteristically incensed about Libroterr's popular entertainment. The other laughed and asked Jirro, what he wanted: the whole world after all is perverse, and besides, they should stick to physics. Perverse: Jirro had never heard this word before, and when it was explained to him he found it so appropriate that he rechristened the gulley behind the Great Ring—no longer the "street of revelation," it became his "street of perversions." Jirro thoughtfully applied the plural in the intention of thinking systematically through the various kinds of deviances to determine which were the worst, and which of the worst ones in principle were in turn the worst ones in practice. But he never had the free time to be so thorough, deciding instead to simply think of each scene as the worst until he found one worse, all the while using "worse" to refer to a greater degree of something that he could not quite define, although the word "alienation" came close.

That worst scene remained the worst for a long time; neither the clacking conversation of two skeletons as they hacked away at an old man until he looked like them (another entry in the science program "Anatomy for Children") playing at the same time as a beginner's course in cello and an ad from a protein concern warning against food containing too many carbohydrates, nor the graphically displayed embrace of a female gorilla comforting and bucking up the boy she has kidnapped (series: "From the Ancient Archives"), no, none of them could displace the death by poison gas, at least not as far as Jirro was concerned. His interest faded, bit by bit; a sensational construction project (the so-called mountain factory of a certain Moritz Cornelius Asher) consumed his full attention, and at the same time something disappointing came to trouble this hobby of his: the summer programming arrived, with its gentle music and sweet nothings, its whispered promises and breathy kisses that drowned out the words, and so Jirro discovered that age-old formula to please: gunsmoke, the beating of hooves, the smack of fists against jaws in honest fights of man against man, which the good guy always won, all followed by the happy sound of laughter, without variation, always in the exact same sequence, and this from window to window on every floor; Jirro stopped listening.

And so the "street of perversions" was only a memory that Jirro cultivated with growing melancholy. His time in Libroterr was coming to a close; already the last week, then came the last day, and already tomorrow he would be on the streets of Uniterr, free of predator ads, gangsters, prostitutes, back in his homeland where he would never find a street of perversions. This was Uniterr's mission: to preserve a humanity free of such deviance. Was Jirro proud of his clean country? Oh, every departure brings sentimentality and distorts how we think of the place we are leaving behind. When, lost in reminiscence, Jirro walks the now-familiar streets for the final time, he closes himself off from them, just as he closes his ear to the sounds filling the air, he forgets his morality, and does not think of his homeland.

An early morning; pink dawn, and Jirro wallows in memory: there, from that green-purple (in Libroterr windows and doors were sealed by light-blocking screens that were only transparent from the inside) window had come the first cry that had startled him so; from the gold one up there came the thunder; there on the left the clacking skeletons; and as obvious as it was (or wasn't) that Jirro would move quickly past the scene of the worst incident, it was just as odd, then, that he pauses there, deep in thought, where the memory of footfalls returns to him, now when he can no longer really hear those images which were all the more life-like because he never saw them, and he loses himself in his imagination. It is as though he himself is rushing down that tunnel with someone right behind him. He sees the walls of grey concrete, the low-hanging ceiling, the gate, he sees glassy drops of light, and he also sees the applauding crowd as if behind a haze of flowing iron —

When it happens that a familiar voice calls to him from a window and he is startled nearly to death, as he once was by a bicycle bell. He stands unconscious of his surroundings for a moment, supporting himself on the wall. Then the everyday sounds of Libroterr return to him: the whir of helicopter taxis, violins and soft cries from the windows, and, realizing that the call was not meant for him, another question comes to Jirro: who in Libroterr tunes in to Uniterr's sole television station? Is it someone who doesn't like the summer programming either? Is it a coincidence? Or is it —

And Jirro stands still, in shock at the unmistakable voice of the most beloved actress of his country, one of the few female members of the highest freedom council, recipient of all the highest orders, chair of the council of theater workers, the perfect embodiment of the thoughts and feelings of the best of Uniterr, the essence of that holy mission to defend Uniterr from all deviance, known there as "the soul of the better half of this world." Jirro hears her pronounce that sentence from the consecrated performance that no less a man than the leader of the highest freedom council called "the finest expression of Uniterr's world-historical mission," the sentence that every citizen of Uniterr knows by heart and that Jirro could recite in his sleep—

And as if sleeping, dreaming this familiar sound, Jirro is home again, his homeland appears to him just as he had left it: the tunnel deep under Uniterr's border, through which he had been so proud to be one of those select few permitted to pass, and he sees the walls of grey concrete and the automatic gates, which on command can seal the tunnel, or narrow it, or transform it into a labyrinth, or open trap doors; and he sees the path sloping slowly downward, the words of comrade gatekeeper still in his ears, reminding him of Uniterr's mission. But this is the street of perversions, and all is confusion and deviance: at the very moment when he can see his fatherland and hear that comforting sentence, the thought comes to Jirro that he could easily stay here: in this country, in this city, in this street, and he stands there, once again unconscious of his surroundings—

And for a moment almost succumbing to the deviant thought, he hears the end of the sentence and he hears it in the midst of the everyday sounds of Libroterr, and suddenly this sentence strikes him as the worst of all that he has encountered on this street: *comrade, even if it takes years, we will discuss it with you until you too have been convinced.*

And Jirro, waking from his helplessness, hears the steely sound of the comforting voice and knows as from a revelation that it was broadcast to reach him, in the hour of his worst confusion, deep at the bottom of a darkening chasm over which no sky stretches, it seems to him as though an eye sees him and reads his most private thoughts. As quickly as he can, he runs to his apartment, packs his things, and is ready.

The Duel

Back in the days when he was still toiling away on his causology degree, the insight came to Pavlo, as it sometimes does, that the laws of causality should also be manifest in the history of humanity. So he decided, which was still possible at the time, to audit a few history seminars in addition to his mandatory courses in disciplines of philosophy and state consciousness. He chose a series of lectures about the development of the legal system in the late middle ages, because he had high expectations of an era in which such eminent causal thinking as that of the Romans began to unfold in an environment structured altogether differently from that of Roman law.

At first he was deeply disappointed: the lecturer lost himself in the details of local customs and traditions that had been passed down over time. His lecture was dry, the material even more so, and instead of exposing causal chains, he uncovered only confusion.

Pavlo had already resigned himself to dropping out when the lecturer announced that, for the next hour, he would be performing an ocular demonstration of history with the use of a chronoview cabinet. The device was still in testing at the time, both technically and politically. The supreme council on comradeship (SuCoC) of Uniterr had decided to allow the use of such demonstrations in schools, and perhaps even, as was the dream of a few committee members, to be used as an educational form of public entertainment, to study the effects of the device on a specific audience. That the committee would later distance itself from every public chronoview display can probably be attributed, as we know now, to the outcome of this very experiment in that history seminar.

Technically, the device relied on the primitive, though at that time unique, method of catching up with light that had been beamed into space from past ages, through the use of an ultrafast gravitational wave which would mirror the image back towards Earth at an accelerated rate. As a result, the reflection of times gone by, slowed down again to the speed of light, would revisualize inside a projection space in the present, somewhat like a movie scene, three dimensional, in colour, but silent. A technique that could filter out every sound wave belonging to each light stream, untangling it and making it audible, was only discovered later, as was an analog technique to rediscover scents. Nevertheless, during Pavlo's student days, each chronoview image, however incomplete, still stirred such a sensation that tickets were scalped for almost as much money as for the boxing championships.

Since the announcement of the ocular demonstration, the auditorium had been besieged by curious faculty members from all departments, while the university was overrun by crowds of amateur historians. The campus police only admitted regular attendees; they had to check upstairs about Pavlo. Thanks to his impeccable character references attesting to his loyalty, and his exemplary academic performance, the apprehensive Ministry decided to grant him permission.

For the demonstration they had chosen the famous episode of the duel between the Duke of Normandy, Henri VII of Traulec, and his bastard son Toul, who, sired with a maid, was considered of lesser birth. Little was known about the duel in question, which happened in May of 1409, except that the outcome had been exceptionally gruesome. The duel had come about after Duke Henri ignored his son's objections and relegated him to a life as a lowly swineherd in his father's pigpens. Jeanne Viole du Mars, personal favorite of the royal commissary, took the duke's entirely ordinary judgment as justification for spreading the rumor that Toul had, in accordance with his station as a half-blood, decided to challenge the duke to a duel, which the latter had refused out of cowardice. When whispers of the story reached Toul, standing in the middle of his father's pigs, he decided on the spot to turn rumor into reality; he sent two seconds, who happened to be swineherds like himself, to deliver a challenge to his sire who now had little choice but to consent to the duel, albeit under the stipulation that, as the prevailing law demanded, the conditions for the duelists would be in accordance with their birth. The lowborn man was to be buried up to his hips in a hole in the ground, armed only with a spear and a club, while the highborn man would be given his sharp sword, and the freedom to move without restriction.

There was no wiggle room within the stipulation; whether Jeanne Viole had known about the clause, or indeed, why she started the rumor in the first place, has, as we know, been the subject of entire libraries worth of clever hypotheses. We do know that she was a mortal enemy of Duke Henri, and had supposedly been carried away by the profound ugliness of the bastard (he was hunchbacked, leather-skinned, his face permanently marred by a grimace, and he walked with a limp). There is no doubt that the duel had taken place. Aside from that, no other facts had survived the ravages of time, not even the fate of the protagonist during the domestic chaos under Charles le Fou, the mad king Charles the Sixth of France.

The most significant sources describing the duel are the valuable fragments of the "Luciferian Calendar" by Estienne Nouvielles, as well as the much later and unfortunately highly fragmented Annals of the "Unknown Chronicler of the Duchy". In addition there remain a few letters from Jeanne Viole and the other courtiers, a couple of references in other letters, and a handful of diary scraps. In those days, the world was entranced by the Council of Pisa with its three popes, the reverberations of the murder of the duke of Orleans in Paris, and the sermons of Jan Hus in Bohemia. Furthermore, the English were about to invade France once again, so why would a third rate mistress be the subject of local intrigue? The duel only became famous by virtue of its mysterious outcome, described only as "exceptionally gruesome", a pithy statement that inflamed historians. One hypothesis, which seemed to draw analogies to the court of Charles the Mad, envisioned a fire in which both combatants died; another theory that was particularly in vogue posited a riot among the local citizens of Traulec. The doctrine in Uniterr has always been that the swineherd defeated the duke, although the hack writers of the ruling caste hushed up the truth, a prime example of the intellectual servitude that dominated the past and that was only overcome in Uniterr, which was so certain of its own doctrine that it showed up in every schoolbook as though it were fact.

This shift from fiction to fact is part of the philosophy of history in Uniterr, but before we say any more about that, and before we finally tell you about that demonstration, the outcome of which was indeed gruesome, we should say something about the technical aspect of the process: The projection field was almost invisible, though still clearly observable as a shimmering room no higher than 6 feet, and only 10 feet long and wide. Thus, at a scale of fifty to one, a historical scene of about 500 feet long and wide, and 300 feet into the sky could be captured. As a result, the actors only measured an inch, a society the size of ants. A system of magnifying lenses made it possible for viewers to choose any section of the panorama and view it in detail right before their eyes, as if through a microscope. And a camera would of course record every scene on a real-life scale. It goes without saying that the projection process could no more be controlled by the audience than they could manipulate the image of the stars in the sky through the lens of their eyes.

So Pavlo was given permission to participate, and since admission had opened up several hours before the start of the demonstration, he missed nothing while they checked up on him. The soft purring of the oscillators; the slowing down from the super speed of the mirrored light too place far away along an avenue of satellites. Had an uninitiated person entered the lecture hall, he would have noticed nothing but a grey platform on the demonstration table, with three cables each as thick as an arm, and above it a barely visible angular shimmering. Yet soon he would notice that pervasive tension of curiosity, that irredeemable human right, all around the room. This curiosity was, above all, a desire for raw sensation; that feeling you experience before a boxing match, knowing you have come there to see something unbridled and rough, ending in broken noses and the booming sound of a man crashing unconscious to the floor. These were the expectations that brought men and women together. For Pavlo, well, perhaps we'll get back to that later. The purring of the oscillators grew stronger, the shimmering of the helium wires, fading into the dawn light, became the quivering aura of the tidings that the two-thousand year old light was about to return home to its planet. As flashes dispersed from the edges with silent humility, Pavlo was seized by an ineffable feeling that all that was to come was already present.

Pavlo felt a sense of expectation, more gripping than any he had ever known, and somehow entirely different in nature from the feeling that word usually evokes. This was not the anticipation of the familiar (the way a child waits for his fairytale), but that of an entirely new sensation, which, grotesquely, is also a past sensation. So an unknown sensation, not unknown in the sense that the brain has not yet narrowed down the feeling from a supply of familiar sensations, no, this was something absolutely new, or, to be precise at last: the possibility of the unknown. It did not enter the conscious mind as a concept: it was an imminent necessity, which presented itself as a necessary lack of alternative, something that the mind cannot conceive of at all, and all the same it made Pavlo tremble.—Only him?—We'll assume so; if not, let him serve as a case in point for his flock of peers. Though it did actually happen to him alone.

The purring of the oscillators ceased, or rather: the sound transformed into a reverberation which, wavering on the verge of the audible, was not quite perceptible as background noise, nor did it turn into hollow silence. As we said earlier, the chronoview technology was still in the early stages of its development, unable to reproduce the original sound; the reverberation, despite being inaudible, created a soundscape before which the oppressively uncanny muteness of history began to unfold its secret. That reverberation, which sounded like silence, was a positive rather than a negative nothingness; and with the start of the reverberation, the shimmering was no longer visible either, or, to be precise again: it was no longer noticeable now that the past had materialized above the grey platform, unimaginably abrupt. Under the weight of a steel sky, a crowd of thousands lined the block of North Sea air. So the distant past settled on the desk, while the spectators turned and twisted their macroscopes to focus on the details they wanted to see, while outside the operators of the time stream cameras were struggling to find the perfect angle for a wide shot. To get a good view of the duelists, who were concealed by the masses, the cameramen kept changing positions; the crowd broke up—We'll now tell you the story as Pavlo saw it.

For a moment he surveyed the scene: How tremendous the sky! A towering mass of clouds, wind, and shades of blue. Below, along the periphery, the human throng as a colourful maelstrom that resists the dragging weight of the sky and thus reveals its violence: eternity persisting in change, a bastion of constancy over the fleeting life of man. The cameras panned out, Pavlo saw colours and solid shapes inside the cube; finally he too began to twist his macroscope and as the image grew and turned, the lady appeared before his eyes.

She stood before him, and Pavlo's breath caught. He saw her, nearly close enough to feel her breath; she came closer and turned slightly sideways, revealing the burnt umber pattern woven through her sea-green brocade; her head and neck rose up from her rounded cleavage like the isles of the Sirens. Her scarlet cap pointed towards the sky, and the night dwelled in her eyes. She approached her observer; Pavlo could almost feel her milky skin. He saw her in the flesh, as though he needed no lens, and then she vanished through his face. Behind her in the dust was a dwarf, who ran crying after her mistress. The massive wet flesh of her tongue was grotesque; Pavlo wrested his macroscope away; a donkey's hoof.

Now the cameras locked on the opponents: There was the back of the duke, who pranced around with his legs spread apart, wearing the fashion reserved for the nobility of the age, the renowned mi-parti: A doublet divided into four solid panels, alternating two colours on the front, as well as on the back; green and black in this case, with puffed sleeves tapering towards the wrist. Similarly divided into panels were his tight pants and the curly-toed poulaines with their green-and-black tassels. Even the feathers on his red cap were green and black, the colours of the banner of Traulec.—His sword, tied low, skipped through the dust.—Sloping away from him was the pit in which Toul stood, up to his waist in crumbling dirt, which was as brown as his wart-covered face with that monstrous nose, its flesh spilling over like a mockery of God's power of creation. His weapons were nowhere to be seen; he raised his bare hands and laughed, as Pavlo spotted, across the bustling crowd, the scarlet cone of the lady's headdress. Only now did he notice that she was on horseback. She was seated at a slight angle on a palfrey; the treading of the horse made her seem like a giant, the colour of the sea, striding through the crowd. Pavlo was confused as never before. Anxiously twisting and turning he tried to bring the lady close to him again, but he saw, through the growing crowd, no more than a trace of her robe, which at once disappeared again between steel and silk. Focusing on those glimpses Pavlo perceived only objects: a row of jasper buttons, a spur, a sable purse, but not the lady, or the duke, or Toul, or the courtiers whom Pavlo had briefly spotted in front of the sea of blue around the Fleur de Lis of France, raised on a stage beyond the fight.

He lowered the shaft of his macroscope, and saw the bottom layer of the chronoview cabinet, which resembled fine lace. The people at the front were still recognizable as individuals. He was bursting with excitement, a sensation due less to the presence of Jeanne Viole, whose scarlet headdress bobbed further towards the sky, than by—and we cannot say this often enough—the potential for any possible outcome, a potential as boundless as yearning could be, when given proper room for growth. Within the structure of the one truth lay the possibility of possibilities, as a possibility of the other: For the first time in his life, Pavlo experienced a sense of being struck by something intangible which, eluding all words, dawned on him with all the horror and pleasure of a premonition. This ancient history could and might turn out to be different from Uniterr's account of history, something unexpected.

But what had Pavlo expected to see?

He could not have articulated it yet at the same time he knew, and therein lies the difficulty.

Like his fellow students, Pavlo believed, obviously, the official hypothesis that was part of Uniterr's doctrine, namely that of Toul's victory, which had been covered up by medieval chroniclers. This, on the one hand. On the other hand, to accept the victory of an inferior man over his superior stood in direct contradiction to the official doctrine of history in Uniterr, which held that, before the creation of the truly liberated society, all historical events served to benefit the upper classes. That meant that all events had a predetermined outcome, which had led to numerous suppressed uprisings by an increasingly angry population. Uniterr was the first, and sadly the only one thus far, to have erected a truly liberated society in which social inequality had ceased to exist. Its doctrine ("the truly truthful history") was so widely accepted that the state was no longer aware to what extent it wrote its own facts. The official doctrine offered the only acceptable model for historical thinking, and in most cases it did so at the expense of any kind of demonstrability. As a result, Pavlo and his fellow students, lacking introspection, were certain that the outcome of a duel like this, between a superior and his inferior, must have been predetermined in favor of the superior. And in the event that the fight's natural course went in the wrong direction, that is, if the duke were not the fitter competitor, then marshals, his seconds, and the jury would secure the victory of the superior through deceptive manipulation. (No doubt they had planned out a thousand strategies to distract or obstruct the Bastard.) The official claim of Toul's victory and the official doctrine about the rigging of events in favor of the upper classes were incompatible; so what was Pavlo expecting? If we don't consider the word 'expectation' in the sense of a concrete, demonstrable imagining (which was entirely unknown in Uniterr), but rather in the sense of a predetermined certainty that something will happen—we could also call it a 'lack of expectation', then he may have expected both outcomes at once. Only in an abstract sense though, not concrete, and since that option lacked an element of demonstrability, he did not notice any inherent contradiction either. That may sound hard to believe, yet it was true, or rather: that is how it will be. Let us tell you, what happened in the future.

The state of abstract certainty in which one expects nothing was disrupted by the unexpected, which, to say it a third time, was the possibility of any and all possibilities as a reality of the other. The concrete, by virtue of being concrete, is already other to the abstract, just as the verifiable is other to the unverifiable. Where history presents itself as other, it has already become, in its appearance, the same as at its core: The existence of alternatives. The slightest detail gains meaning, which can only be understood by those who have experienced it. That it was possible to wear a scarlet headdress reaching to the sky—Not that it would be illegal in Uniterr, it just wouldn't spontaneously occur to anyone to make such an unbidden fashion choice.—That it was possible to ride a palfrey; that it was possible to appear in a costume that bisects the body into two colours, one sleeve of which was tailored while the other billowed; that it was possible to drink wine from a clay jug; that it was possible for a sword to skip through the dust; that it was possible to wield a sword; that it was possible to drive a donkey; that it was possible to be stuck in a hole in the ground and bare your teeth at the authorities –

That it was possible not to be Uniterr.

The crowd parted and suddenly even the impossible, or rather, precisely the impossible seemed possible to Pavlo: that an emperor could rise from a gridiron, that the earth slowly folded itself into mountains, that fish marched across land, that wings could sprout from human shoulders, that horses could cast off their tack, that the sea-green lady could bare herself and the elm trees lining the road could bow before her—the lady, left arm leaning on a suit of armor, leapt from her horse.

Meanwhile, Pavlo had tuned his macroscope to create a diorama, framed on the left by the duke and on the right by Toul. The cameras shot from above, at a slight angle, so that the auditorium had a clear view of the scene of the fight. And now it became clear who held the advantage: The crowd surrounding Toul in his pit was so dense that the duke, now drawing his two-hander, looked practically shunned by his entourage. Heralds, trumpets on their hips, went before the courtesan, paying their respects to the nobility; an armed guard carries spear and truncheon, the dwarf curtsied as the man passed; and the lady approached Toul.

Pavlo felt overwhelmed by the scene, and now the thought inspectors, observing the demonstration from their headquarters (of course) began to notice as well: The emotiograph in the auditorium detected a sudden influx of neuron vapor, the prime indicator of rising excitement. The bright blue light, blinking well outside of acceptable ranges, signaled a dangerous emotional build-up overriding individual awareness control. That dysfunction, first observed on this occasion, was later dubbed "alternative syndrome", and it was categorized as a schizoid anomaly. A precautionary alert was sent to the SuCoC.

The lady crouched down by the pit; behind her, the dwarf clapped wildly as the lady, gathering the seam of her skirt, unbuttoned the top of her robe and drew from its ambiguous depths a small woven sack of gold from which she fed Toul a large, yellow-brown chunk of rock candy. She slipped it into his snapping mouth; between Toul's eyes and hers lay a shadowy white chasm. The lady laid her hands on Toul's face, holding him by his chin and nose, and drew the rent cleft so close to her own lips that Pavlo felt like the courtesan should intervene. The hum of silence in the auditorium; soundless trumpets blowing, halberds forcing back the crowd, and between the adversaries, the gaping void seemed to drag down the sky itself. In a single grand movement, a ribbon of dark weather swept through the violent firmament. A swarm of blackbirds took flight and disappeared in the far distance across the sea, - Toul, now alone, licked his lips with a grin; scarlet flowed towards the stage, and the half-moons of the halberds formed a jagged grid across the horizon.

The lights in the control room, which had been flashing blue like a feverish sky as Jeanne Viole crouched before the pit, had calmed down again and the graphs registered normal levels. The Inspectors breathed a sigh of relief. As the adversaries reverentially traced the sign of the cross across their bodies, from forehead to navel, the courtesan delivered the opening proclamation: *Ad te in excelsior domine clamavi*, a well-known expression.—His fingers sparkled blue: a polished sapphire, turquoises, opals, an amethyst suspended in a narrow gold channel, a grandiose aquamarine, and behind him the royal blue enveloping the lilies of this mad ruler. The four umpires who had entered the arena strode around garbed in blue, like towers of faith in tradition and law. The loam-brown battlefield, the duke in green and black, Toul's face, brown like the dirt in which he was buried; the crowd a teeming mass of colour. A sword pierced the scarlet. Using both hands, the duke raised the sword to the skies from his billowing and tapered sleeves, each quartered into green and black like his doublet and pants. Nestled between green and black lay the enormous bulge of his pomegranate-like codpiece, lined with bells and woven from seven cloths. He arched his back to keep his sword pointing up at the sky; he held the steel with outstretched arms, and Pavlo thought he could see the reflection of the Castle of Traulec glowing in the curve of the man's back; that—as enthusiasts called it later—fortified Wonder of the West, (which nonetheless melted during the four-millisecond atomic pacification of the rebels of Saint-Lô).

Although the duel was about to start, the blue lights in the control room were dead; the spectators were definitely trembling with excitement, but their anticipation was within the norm; the excitement drained away as quickly as it rose, and it did so in a normal manner: People shifted in their seats, crossed the other leg, cleared their throats, laughed, hollered in jest, cheered for the contestants, whispered intimacies to the people from past centuries as they twisted them closer, and even for those whose excitement did not develop into outward articulation, the tension dissipated entirely within their consciousness. Even from Pavlo's corner nothing disconcerting was transmitted through the emotiographs, which of course allowed for the detection of localized distress. In front of the inspectors lay a seating plan of the auditorium, and at the first flash of a blue light they had promptly exclaimed: "That new guy after all!" Now the inspectors finally gave in to the joy of watching the spectacle, almost entirely without concern. Perhaps it was a matter of habit, ingrained in the body (or mind), that more than watching the competitors, their eyes were on the crowd that thrust itself against the halberds guarding the imposing stage: Richly coloured pageantry, leather and fustian, raw pelts, thick linens, bodies girdled by enormous belts, horned headdresses wedged into one another, and faces basking in unbridled joy.—The inspectors disapproved of them being armed, long knives or short swords, some wide-bladed spears, even a couple of crossbows and quivers with bundles of feathered arrows; it was degenerate and brazen. Many ate as they gawked, a wine flask made the rounds. The inspectors disapproved of that too.—What made them happy was the noble attitude of the duke, who still stood bent under the might of his steel. They barely looked at Toul in his pit. The latter protruded, brown from the brown dirt, in his left hand a spear, in his right a bludgeon, staring towards the stage on which silver brocade and silk were gathered around the representative of the crown. To the left of the courtesan was a gap and Pavlo, who had followed Toul's gaze, expected the lady to appear on the stage at any moment, milky flesh and skin like the sea, with her hidden cocoon made of gold. The scarlet had disappeared from the sky, which was still dominated by the towering sword. Seagulls swooped through the ribbon of weather and Pavlo longed, more than anything in the world, to see Jeanne Viole one more time.

He had lost all interest in the duel, along with the ceremonies and rituals accompanying the fight. As he stared into the crowd's surge of colours, he remembered that intangible touch, as she slid across his face, followed by the dwarf with her wet tongue, but now he couldn't spot either. There did seem to be an occasional opalescent hint of sea green breaking through the chaos, and Pavlo would greedily swing his macroscope in that direction: Why couldn't humans be born with compound eyes like a fly? Why hadn't anyone invented a device that let you see in every direction at once? He peered across the crowd between the stage and the pit, the way a hunter stalks through a corn field, waiting for the twitch of a stalk to betray his prey as it pushed invisibly through the rows. Only now did he see what the inspectors had seen from the beginning: that the crowd was armed, and that they gawked, and laughed, and Pavlo thought he must be dreaming, and that he could make the lady reappear in his dream if only his desire were strong enough. He twisted and turned the wheel as if he could transform history with his fingers, yet the paunch that obscured his view refused to move even an inch; its massiveness seemed to mock him. The paunch wore a violet robe. The man stood there as if he could taste the irritation that his vastness caused the distant spectators, and Pavlo, awakened too soon from his dream, realized he was utterly powerless to control the past—in this moment he decided, though he didn't know it then, to become an inventor, and learn to look into the future.

A monk sprinkled holy water on the duke. The crowd roared inaudibly.—A sudden crush formed in front of the stage, a jug of wine or beer shattered against the ground, even the violet paunch had disappeared. Behind the corsets, closing the gap that he had left, Pavlo spotted a bright flash of white from a pelt; the pigeons plunged towards the ground, and the duke lowered his sword. His body mimicked the gesture as though he was greeting the bastard with the lowering of his sword. Pavlo, trying to bring the palfrey back into sight, twisted his macroscope to maximum magnification, and there appeared the face of the dwarf, peeping out from between the hips of two women. She looked around, turned sharply to the side to expose her profile, narrow watery eyes underneath a forehead with plucked brows, devoid of lashes, a naked, wet eye. Pavlo suddenly felt like history itself, in the flesh, was looking him in the eyes, shameless, exposed, and unfathomable, with an air of apathetic treachery. The eye turned directly toward him. Nothing but this eye, the floating void of the pupil, stripped of eyelashes under a browless, hairless forehead. The hips closed in on each other so that Pavlo saw nothing but the borderless eye, and then only the cloudy bottomlessness; he was sucked into the oval void, greedily indulging in his horror so that the lady was all but forgotten. Within this eye there seemed to rest the entirety of all possibilities one dared not dream about, though we dream them every night, as eager as we are terrified of what dreaming makes real, and sleep consigns to oblivion. The hips pushed together, purple and tan, seamlessly overlapping, but Pavlo did not release his piercing stare as a wedge of scarlet glided along the dragging sky. He thought he could still see the center of the bottomless depth that was the eye, in a poppy seed dot, between the waists covered by flowing sleeves; a pure black leading into the depths of all desire. Only when the violet paunch covered the purple and tan once more did the obsessed man turn back to the tournament, looking at the stage along with the rest of the crowd. Next to the courtesan stood the lady, surrounded by dancers honoring the royal party, and only now did he notice that she too was browless, a face painted smooth.—She smiled and Pavlo sought her eye, terrifyingly isolated by nothingness. It lay on the lectern, lashless and grotesque, and suddenly Pavlo saw death within the eye, a black and concave skull, naked. A terrifying, dreaming embryo. He flinched. Iridescent sea green, from which the tip of a poulaine emerged, scarlet like the tip pointing to the sky; then the scarlet slipped back underneath the sea.

The flurry of brocade and silver settled. The duke, approaching the stage, took off his cap to honor the faraway king in a movement that reached deep into the room. Trumpets flew up to meet lips, and, their expectations confirmed, the inspectors in the control room looked on with a nod of approval as the crowd pushed forward once more towards the almost gracefully commanded barrier of halberds. At that moment, Toul pulled himself up, clearly making a racket since he drew the attention of the entire crowd, and Pavlo's as well, just as Jeanne Viole, bending down over her dwarf, slid a piece of rock candy into his mouth. One pair of eyes towering above the other, the women now turned to watch Toul as well. Toul pulled himself up out of his pit, and, dropping his spear and truncheon, he tore open the bulge under his doublet with both hands, and curving his back dramatically, he pulled out his raw and red swollen member, pointing it towards the royal stage where the duke was delivering his formal greeting to the King. And before the silent spectator of the distant future could break into a public display of horror, a voice rang out above the whirring, as if the King of France himself had used his powers to break through the silence of history. It was an order to shut down the transmission; the scene instantly vanished. Darkness and utter silence; gone the reverberations, extinguished the shimmer.

The duty professor immediately realized that the transmission had been halted at the command of the SuCoC (he thought he'd recognized the voice of a Comrade who was in charge of Safety Services). In order to salvage the embarrassing situation (and it was embarrassing), the professor knew he had to break the silence right away, so as he turned the lights back on, standing in front of the empty cocoon of wires on his desk, he began to present a clinical analysis of what they had witnessed: They had been, so he explained, directing his voice at one of the emotiographs (which also carried sound waves of course), they had been eye witnesses to the affirmation of Uniterr's Science of History, which had proven itself in a magnificent way. Suddenly a voice rang out through the auditorium: "No!"

The professor spun around.

"No," said Pavlo a second time, now standing up.

The entire auditorium stared at the unknown student as though he were the continuation of the spectacle. The duty professor stood paralyzed as though he had just seen a tree rise up from the ground and run away on its roots. He, who was renowned for his resolve and quick wit in debates, he found himself shaken by a single word, as shaken as the doctrine he taught. This "No!" when there could only have been a "Yes," this utterly unimaginable "No," could, yes, provoke the unimaginable. It was a provocation like no other and it made the duty professor sick to his stomach. He felt his knees buckle, dark spots clouded his vision, a buzzing filled his ears and he had to grab the desk to keep himself from falling. In doing so, he accidentally grabbed the chronoview cabinet and he could feel the network of wires in his hand, he sensed that they held him up, and the only thing he could think about was the comrades of the SuCoc, who might be watching him, seeing his failure to honor the great trust they had put in him. They probably were.

We cannot know exactly what happened, since nothing leaves the SuCoC room. But we know what the controllers thought, and how they thought the same thing the professor now did in his helpless despair: namely that something needed to be done at once. The 'at once' part was indisputable. This "No!" was not merely an objection, it was the concentration of all conceivable (no, actually, inconceivable) objections, and worse still: it was the ultimate rejection, the denial of all the affirmation in the word "Yes!" as a yes to Uniterr. A single "No!" was as impossible as a "How?" without a point of reference; it could only mean concrete rejection: "No to Libroterr's pseudo-scientific heresy!"—"No to Libroterr's pessimistic philosophy of history!"—"No to the demon of denial!"

Yet here was this "No!" in its naked pretension of being the alternative to every "Yes!"—The professor's stomach turned to ice. He had never feared challenges or questions about a particular thesis, nor doubts about the facts surrounding a case or allusions to supposed antinomies in his lectures. All of these objections could be steered towards a "Yes!" if you only knew how to handle them. They focused on details, trying to test him, and even in their questioning they remained within the ranks of the sciences, the way the poison of a vaccine remains contained within the system of a healthy person. But this "No!" was a contamination, or worse: a concentration of all possible viruses, from which unimaginable outbreaks were bound to burst forth. And precisely such an outbreak of the unimaginable struck the professor before anyone else: the rippling darkness that had threatened to engulf him now ebbed away, and for one long moment, he believed he could see, in the wires of the Chronoview Cabinet, Uniterr's most senior comrades standing on the stage, dressed in blue from head to toe, pointing their fingers at him, the professor, while beckoning a black and green executioner with a shining sword. The word "No!" was emblazoned on the front of the stage. Now the professor cried out too! Was he just imagining it or had he really just yelled "No!" right into the ears of the SuCoC?

The shock of these horrors startled the professor back into awareness, just as the head of the controllers had decided to order the auditorium evacuated, and just as he had formulated his command in his mind. So startled was the professor, that the only way he could think of to neutralize that "No!" was to turn its own power against it, and so, climbing onto his desk, he shouted out in a piercing voice "No!"

All eyes were on him.

"Yes?" asked Pavlo, unsure of what had come over him - The duty professor took this as a sign of surrender, when it was merely the confusion of someone who discovers, in the process of finding himself, that he is simultaneously losing himself.

Pavlo had never intended to speak up; his "No!" had felt like it came from a stranger. As if in a dream, the word had slipped through the gap between his lips, from his mouth which had involuntarily hung open since the moment the first image was transmitted into the auditorium. He was deeply disturbed by this sense of otherness. At first, he wanted the feeling to last forever: to be different from Uniterr! Pavlo experienced this "No!" as in a dream; incomprehensible that someone in the auditorium could say something like that, and unbelievable that he had been the one to say it. But now it was out there, and it had already begun to change him, the one who had introduced it into Uniterr's reality. To understand this "No!" as *his* "No!" To realize its significance with respect to the truth values of Uniterr's Truly Truthful Theory of History (and to have an inkling of the consequences). Still as if in a dream, he raised himself from his seat, and saw a life-sized Toul pull himself out of his pit, stretching towards his opponents, fueled by a raging lust for vengeance. In his desire to emulate Toul, though he shuddered to think about it, Pavlo had exclaimed his second "No!" with instinctual determination. Appalled, he came back to his senses and realized that he *had* behaved like the man who had now faded into the flickering light. In the eyes of his fellow students, who stared at him in unison, Pavlo saw the abyss. The professor's "No!" had pushed him over the edge. He was rapidly plunging towards his fate, bewildered, incredulous, unbroken. He'd been thrust from a dream into a terrifying nightmare, and dragged through the horror as though in a dream. He had nearly said yes to all the no's, a yes that might carry him through. And he did feel carried, floating on the stares that focused on him with the same raw curiosity that they had directed at the flesh of the bygone era, eager for an eruption of violence and bloodshed.

Let us share with you what Pavlo didn't see. The historical scenes were still being beamed down by the team up in space, as nobody had given them orders to halt the transmission. The receivers in the SuCoC and the control room revealed how the guards knocked Toul back into the pit; how, at the same time, the crowd doubled up with laughter, and the violet paunch tossed his hat into the sky, and a donkey kicked the side of the stage, and the duke swung his sword through the air, and Jeanne Viole blew a kiss to the competitor down in the pit. As this all transpired, and as the professor, already basking in his triumph and swelling with the pride of an epic champion, bellowed out his second "No!" as a "No to this unbelievable insolence!", Pavlo thought he recognized, within his own transformation, the possibility of transforming Uniterr as well. Convinced of this possibility, he announced, in a blissful state of conscious dreaminess, that he was requesting a scientific dispute.

The rest of this story is short, but before we finish it, we must explain to our readers what a scientific dispute is, or rather, what it will be.

The scientific dispute (*scidis*) is defined in the statutes of the united universities of Uniterr as the "preeminent example of the significance of a true battle of opinions for the development of the sciences". They can occur in the form of a scheduled or unscheduled *scidis* (three may be scheduled per academic year). An unscheduled *scidis* serves the scientific processing, penetration, and appropriation of extraordinary events in Uniterr's society". A scheduled *scidis* was executed by the President of the University, while an unscheduled *scidis* had to be sanctioned by the government. An unscheduled *scidis* was committed to film and copies were "incorporated into the National Archive". The "event of a scheduled *scidis*" was confirmed by the Supreme Council of Comrades of the university, while an unscheduled one was confirmed by the Supreme Council of Comrades of the government after which it was "to be declared accepted doctrine by the University President or, respectively, the government."

The professor informed Pavlo that he should propose a theme and a thesis in accordance with the procedure outlined in the statutes, with eight copies to be distributed. Pavlo agreed to do so.

After that, the duty professor declared that the ocular demonstration of history, which had confirmed beyond all doubt the accuracy of the Truly Truthful Sciences, was now over. The students returned to their quarters, each maintaining a respectful distance to Pavlo, and each armed with the steady determination to remain silent during the dispute. They would stick to their decisions.

As soon as Pavlo left the lecture hall, he began thinking about how he could formulate the theme of his proposal, but he couldn't come up with the right approach. What was the point of a "No!" when it wasn't concrete? When it didn't relate to anything that could be denied? And to whom had he directed this

"No!" anyway? To Uniterr? That was impossible. To the Truly Truthful Sciences? The question dissipated. Was he no longer willing to accept the Sciences as truth? His thoughts wandered.

Pavlo and his fellow students walked out into a bright day in May. The sky over Uniterr was blue as far as the eye could see, dotted with swarms of birds. What had been the object of his "No!"? Pavlo considered his question, and discovered the double meaning of the word "object". What had been the object, and what had been his objective? And as he considered his goal, in hopes of finally finding a foothold, he realized he couldn't even identify a goal. The object was as far away as Charles le Fou.

While Pavlo was getting lost in his own questions, the duty professor was given orders to report to the control room, where, as he'd secretly hoped but not expected, the Ocular Demonstration was still playing, and its current phase was so enthralling that the eyes of the controllers were glued to the scene. Since nobody was asking questions and their guest kept mum, there appeared to be consensus from the outset that, instead of addressing the Pavlo situation, they would follow the duke's leap, which had apparently started the duel: The man from Traulec bounds towards the pit in two swift leaps, seemingly unencumbered by his sword, and swings, spinning a full 360 degrees, at Toul's neck, but the latter ducks. The duke sails past the pit, and Toul's bludgeon hits him in the heels with such force that he crashes to the ground, sword and all. Toul goes after him, like a brown flash shooting from the dirt; the guards throw themselves in his path, shoving and kicking him back to his pit. In the process, they block the duke's blow, with which he is trying to sever the furiously squirming man's spine.

At least, that's what the controllers saw through their macroscopes. The professor, still standing by the door (he wouldn't dare sit down without permission), just saw the totality of the miniature scene, the sky and the foreboding sea, the movement of the people like waves flowing through the scene, streams, swirls, lines, circles, ceaselessly changing shapes and colours clustering together and then unraveling. He was so fascinated by the sight that he forgot all about Pavlo.

Meanwhile, the latter was still mulling things over. What had been the object of his "No!"? For the nth time, he replayed in his mind the words of the duty professor, and as they did not change, he tried to recollect what anyone else had said, but he got nowhere. So instead he tried to remember the scene, Toul and the duke, the courtesans and the lady, the people and the guards, the lilies and the sword and the bludgeon, yet instead of visualizing them, he thought about names and he thought about concepts. When he closed his eyes he saw the female dwarf who accompanied the lady, her vacant eye within that smooth, vanishing face.

He gave up. First some sleep! He felt so indescribably tired, he couldn't so much as hope for a dream.

Near the site of the duel, the professor saw people relaxing, crowding around the wine barrels, gathering around the roasting spits full of sausages and the stalls selling bread. There seemed to be unlimited quantities of food and drink, and perhaps for these people, the duel was just a pretext for carefree indulgence.—The scarlet cone dominated the scene; he stood exactly in the center of the battlefield, where the duel, once out of control, had now stagnated in a curious manner: The duke, restrained by guards, had taken a few steps back. Toul, still in the pit, was shaking his fist and his bludgeon and he appeared to be talking to the crowd, who were shaking with laughter; even the guards were now cracking up, the shafts of their halberds bouncing up and down. Toul lifted himself halfway out of the pit again, and shouted something at the stage, where something responded by moving: before the blue of the lily-sky a slowly thickening cloud of steel. - One of the controllers, a specialist, attempted to translate the lip movements of the increasingly wildly gesturing Toul into sounds, but as he didn't know Middle French, he only deciphered meaningless phonemes.

Now the cloud grew to cover the sea-green as well and soon only scarlet remained visible.

The professor, who had kept his eye on a table full of magnifying glasses that weren't being used, contemplated whether he dared sit down at the table. He'd even prepared a justification: he was doing this in the service of Uniterr and for the greater good. Just as he was about to speak up, he realized that it would be inadvisable to disturb the enthralled crowd of controllers at this exact moment, and so he restrained himself and tried to will his eyes to focus on the tiny scene visible through the lenses. The scene now showed a stage, from which the scarlet cone had disappeared.

But the controllers were not looking at the stage, they were looking at the guards on the edge of the pit. Three members of the crowd had approached them: A man, two women, wine, pretzels, and breasts. They offer the guards a drink, which they accept. Perhaps it's fraternization, perhaps a bribe, maybe a plot against the king's men. Toul keeps talking, a guard drinks, a second follows, a third reaches under a woman's skirt, throngs push up against the halberds, another cask is rolled in. Crowds converge on the cask like a whetstone honing a blade. The crowd is closing in at the duke's flank too. Narrow channels split the crowd, like dark rays emanating from the inner ring. Fires blaze in the distance, the cloud on stage grows darker—these were unusual signs, as portentous as the flocks of migrating birds materializing once again in the grey vault overhead, but also in Pavlo's dream.

He hadn't hoped for a dream, in fact, he'd dreaded dreaming. Sleep had come rapidly and quietly, like the sinking of dusk, laced with ribbons of slowly drifting fog, darkening as the night blew in. Ever blacker drafts carried along a message, from which suddenly a raven appeared, plummeting toward the dreamer, who wanted to cry out but couldn't. Raven after raven plummeted towards him, and Pavlo screamed a silent scream until the sky was empty once more, and that's when he saw the sky turn hollow, like a concave pit, in which, slowly drifting towards him, a crevice gradually opened, nothing but a crevice initially, and that's what terrified Pavlo: That hazy grey of the hollow pit; he knew what would slip through the crevice, and at last he heard the sound of his scream.

Meanwhile at the university, as the group of examiners audibly gasped. The professor, determined to finally request a seat at the table, suddenly spotted the scarlet cone again across the commotion around the pit, where one of the women grabbed the halberd of the man penetrating her body underneath the linen. At that very moment, the transmission to the control room was cut off, this time with an official announcement. The controllers were so greatly vexed by this interruption that the four of them made no effort to conceal their displeasure, and yes, even surprise, in front of their guests. They left the professor standing by the door. But having now, for the second time today and in his entire life, heard the voice of the supreme authority making a final decision, history unfolding in intimate proximity, he registered this disrespect as something much greater than a question of manners. He, earwitness to necessity itself, realized with a startling shudder that he too had made history, and that they were permitting him to continue making history. With an unprecedented determination to do even greater justice to his share of the responsibility for Uniterr's future from this day forward, he regarded the controllers' discontent as a form of atonement for his initial failure.

He was hereby ordered, began the head of the controllers, turning his seat away from the transmission device, not to muzzle the unscheduled *scidis*, but rather to ensure it take place under strict regulation, as defined in the statutes.

"Understood," said the professor.

Furthermore, he should know that a special protocol would be put in place for the procedure of the *scidis*, starting with the fundamental particulars: proposal, theme, and extensive thesis.

When was he to submit these particulars?

That sort of thing should not be rushed, he should take his time.

"In two days?" asked the professor?

"Not that much time."

As the professor headed to Pavlo's—where else?—he tried to imagine how the duel had ended, but couldn't. What bothered him was the behavior of the people; it suggested the complete absence of any code of conduct.

Actually, thought the professor, walking beneath the bright blue May sky that wrapped itself around Uniterr, actually that which they had seen was not history at all, but rather a bundle of confusion, an accumulation of coincidences, not worth watching and essentially scientifically non-existent and lacking theoretical significance. If one thing was absolutely certain, it was the utter lack of epistemic value in what they had witnessed. But if it had not been history which they had seen with their own eyes, then what was it? For a brief moment it occurred to the professor that there might be two types of history, one that led to Uniterr, and one that led to Libroterr (as usual he left Andorra, the third state, out of consideration), but then he remembered that the territory of the duke belonged to present-day Uniterr. So history after all then, albeit incorrect. The professor knew he wasn't actually in a position to judge, since he missed out on the most important moment, namely the one that had prompted the Supreme Authority to shut down the control room—What could it have been? Toul's taunt? That remained inaudible—Depravities? That had been the reason the transmission was shut down in the auditorium, but not in the control room. Besides, who could imagine a more unseemly, vulgar gesture than the baring of the male member?—So then what? Riots? The professor paused: Couldn't that, as an act of the people, be considered a positive thing? In an abstract manner: Certainly. In reality? Never. And here he once again heard the gasps of the controllers, four sharp breaths drawn in as one, greedy in their lustful anticipation, resonating with desire for the forbidden—

It is a testament to his education that the professor did not succumb to the unexpected desire that had arisen in him. Aware that he was walking a fine line, he now saw, clear as daylight, how reprehensible his speculation truly was. If the supreme council of comrades had refused even these unwavering guards an opportunity to witness the past, then there must have been reasons, good reasons, valid reasons, reasons that served the greater good of Uniterr. Shouldn't we be doubly, no, triply glad to be protected from something so dangerous that it could harm us through a single glance? How could an unauthorized individual judge its true consequences? To be fortunate enough to be protected, the feeling warmed his heart, how could a fleeting wisp of curiosity outweigh that? The professor understood, now more than ever, that the hunt for the subjective wasn't befitting of Uniterr's scientists; they must align themselves with objective knowledge, which meant that the concrete form of what they had witnessed was irrelevant, only doctrine mattered, and that doctrine remained intact: Toul's victory as a victory of the people.—And that was the direction the *scidis* must take too, this should be the goal of the thesis, which he needed to complete by tomorrow afternoon.

Then a horrible realization washed over him: this deadline was not his, but Pavlo's. And he'd heard nothing about Pavlo's thesis yet except for that grotesque "No!"

Once again everything became a blur, and so despite his expertise in the *scidis*, the professor found himself standing on Pavlo's doorstep, feeling as clueless as Pavlo, who was standing on the other side, unable to go back to sleep. Neither knew how this might end, but both felt inescapably compelled to insist on this *scidis*, despite not knowing its topic.

But when the professor stood face to face with Pavlo at last, and noticed the sheer helplessness on his face, he suddenly knew what needed to be done; and seeing his professor's confidence, Pavlo finally pulled himself together too.

Still standing in the doorway, the professor stated that he had been asked to advise comrade Student that the appropriate committee had come to a consensus and had approved his request. The *scidis* was to be conducted as soon as possible, while the reverberations of the ocular demonstration continued to ripple. The professor was not in the least bit surprised by the ease with which he took control, solving all of his problems. These were extraordinary measures, bypassing the formal proposal and proceedings such as the development of a rationale and a thesis, but they seemed justified, since the *scidis* might take place as early as tomorrow afternoon; a fresh, honest trial of strength. The professor couldn't wait. There was nothing more revitalizing than a truly free display of a truly scientific battle of wits! Valiantly fought, without all the hassle of theses, presentations, and respondents! But, just so they might level the playing field before the battle, perhaps Comrade Student could take this moment to explain the meaning of his "No!"?

Pavlo remained silent; and when the professor, still standing in the doorway, realized how utterly lost Pavlo looked, he continued after a short pause: Presumably Pavlo's "No!" had not been directed at truly truthful history, but rather, at the professor's own comments about the significance of the demonstration. More specifically, he said, comrade student must have realized that this singular demonstration had been unsuitable as an affirmation of the essence of the truly truthful history, and therefore this impulsive "No!" had not been aimed at the theory as such, but rather at a phenomenon of reality long past. Had he understood comrade student correctly?

Pavlo, overwhelmed with gratitude for the professor's true and proper explanation of his "No!" exclaimed "Yes!" The professor left, only to turn around again immediately and make another proposal:

Since they were now in agreement about this "No!", perhaps it would be advisable for him to announce this consensus right at the beginning of the *scidis*; and Pavlo, now absolved of the responsibility of preparing an introduction, immediately said "Yes!" again.

The third "Yes!" came during the *scidis*, though before this could happen, the lady appeared to him once more, shortly after the professor had left. Flowing from his exuberant joy, shimmering sea green and scarlet, her breath clearing the muggy air. "I am your lady!" spoke Jeanne Viole, "I am the lady of your duel! Trust in me and trust in your own courage!"—She smiled at him; and inaudibly she vanished through Pavlo into the wall.

What a day! Pavlo did something he'd never done before. He gathered his spare change, walked into the cafeteria and bought himself a bottle of wine in broad daylight; he even had enough for a second one. He wasn't bothered by the fact that his fellow students were avoiding him. He took it as a sign of silent awe, after all, even he was astonished by this incomprehensible turn of events. Besides, he didn't mind sitting alone. He drank and dreamed of his lady, he saw her in the sea-green of the slender bottle, he saw her in the scarlet of the sinking sun, he saw her in the burnt umber of evening, he saw her luster in the grey wall, and he told her all of the arguments that he would present in tomorrow's battle, and she listened to him until he fell asleep.

The night passed without dreams.

The next afternoon it was time for the *scidis*.

Beaming, Pavlo entered the auditorium, the same auditorium with the same listeners (albeit with a few additional guests of course) as yesterday during the historical demonstration; the same tension; the same silence.

The receiver had been removed; the professor stood behind the lectern. Pavlo sat down at the foot of the podium.

The professor asked the audience for their understanding; in view of the short preparation time, there hadn't been time to announce the theses in advance. And what were the theses? thought Pavlo. But the professor had already launched into his announcement of their consensus regarding Pavlo's "No", which, naturally, did not refer to the truly truthful theory of history, but rather to his, the professor's, concluding comments about the resounding significance of the historical ocular demonstration as the most illustrious confirmation of the truly truthful history. He then asked Pavlo whether the latter agreed with this characterization, to which Pavlo responded with his third "Yes!"

He began to stand up, as he said this, only to sit back down again: sure, he had a thousand explanations for his "No!" tucked away, but he didn't want to squander them all in a premature offensive. He would keep them safely hidden until he'd spied out his opponent's weaknesses, and that's when he would deliver his deadly blow: rational, smiling smoothly, magnanimous. All of this was not so much a consciously chosen tactic for a calculated debate as it was a tribute to his lady, to the figments of his day dreams, the insights inspired by her apparition, the improvisation surrounding the spirit of history; and so his brief rise from his chair was above all a gesture to Jeanne Viole: a spring-loaded surge, a radiant self-exposure, a display of the exalted glow surrounding his being; his sitting down the casual decision not to destroy his opponent quite yet. By lowering himself back into his seat, he granted permission for the spectacle of battle to continue.

So Pavlo settled back down, almost demure. He held his upper arms, as protocol required, tight against his chest, elbows at a right angle, and his lower arms relaxed though without oafishly resting on the lectern with its reading device quote finder. He raised his eyes to the professor, as the rules prescribed, and held up each of his arguments for scrutiny one last time: the gleaming, sharpened sword of the mind, forged before his opponent, whose felling he had delayed so the latter might defend his position, even when it was so blatantly untenable. If the demonstration had proven anything, it was the undeniable contradiction between the Truly Truthful Theory of History and the reality of history itself.

And it did look as though the professor was struggling to defend his position. Standing high above the surrounding audience, which seemed tense with eager silence, he cleared his throat repeatedly, sniffed weightily, then continued speaking: "comrade students, I have-" he cleared his throat again. As he did so, he held between thumb and index finger one of the information cards that controlled the reading device from the podium, a greenish-brown opalescent silicon disk. He slid it into the Reading Machine, and hesitated before pressing "play". Here, he said, speaking as nonchalantly as Pavlo did in his mind, was the SuCoC's official evaluation of the Ocular Demonstration. The demonstration—everyone in the auditorium, including Pavlo, read along—should be considered of immeasurable significance as the most illustrious affirmation of the views of the Truly Truthful Theory of History: it had manifestly, irrefutably, and palpably shown the long-gone dark ages, which Uniterr had finally overcome, as truly dark and truly gone, and therefore fully overcome.

A moment of pure silence crumbled Pavlo's weapons to dust. The professor saw how the exalted glow on the defeated man's face was wiped away by an ashen shade of grey unlike any he'd ever seen.

Overcome with a sense of pity, not without self-interest but pity nonetheless, he spared the vanquished man the admission of defeat and said, once the roaring applause and thunderous stomping of feet had finally faded and students were back in their seats, that he would take the unanimous approval of this entire crowd as a motion and a demand for this *scidis* to continue. This scientific dispute about the unsurpassably accurate, profound, and groundbreaking affirmation of truly truthful history would empower these eager young people to go forth and strive for the highest level of achievement. He then read out the thesis that one of the most eager Comrade Students had spontaneously drawn up for the *scidis* (he named him; more applause). The thesis appeared on the screens; and the *scidis* continued.

After the *scidis*, late in the evening, Pavlo, walking alone through the crowds, returned to the cafeteria to ask for a bottle of wine on credit; even before he spoke, he knew from the dismissive attitude of the comrade tapster on duty what the answer was going to be. Still, he tried. He wanted to see the lady one last time. Yet as he approached the bar, the narrowing of the empty room seemed to squeeze the air out of him like a vise. He stopped, and now the pressure became unbearable. As a soft muttering grew, Pavlo decided to go home. That's when a friend approached him. He was one of the cameramen. He asked if he could speak to Pavlo, in the strictest confidence, about the demonstration they'd seen. He'd hoped to find him here. And when he saw how Pavlo hesitated (the latter only did so as a sign of respect), he invited his friend to join him for a few bottles of wine (his team had received a bonus).

In Pavlo's living cell, in front of the row of bottles, the cameraman finally asked Pavlo directly whether he could explain what precisely had happened in Traulec in 1409. Like Pavlo, he'd seen it, and he'd captured it on film, but he couldn't make sense of what he'd seen.

Neither could he, Pavlo said, taking a sip. Besides, the transmission to the auditorium had been cut off. Had the film crew seen more?

Swearing Pavlo to silence, his friend now told him in a hushed voice what the students, and then the controllers, had no longer been allowed to see: How Toul had been forced back into the pit, and how, as the crowds began to disarm the unsuspecting guards, distracted by wine and the allures of the flesh, the duke had begun hacking into his son with his two-hander, like a madman. Toul had defended himself with his splintering bludgeon, until a long lasso flew over the heads of the guards, capturing the duke like a hare. At that point, the crowds stormed the battlefield and hurled the man from Traulec into the pit, rescuing the flailing Toul, lifting him onto their necks and shoulder, and carrying him past the stage under a sea of blue lily banners billowing above the crowds.

"Under the banner of the king: the people, they'd triumphed—do you understand?" asked the cameraman, and Pavlo shook his head: He understood nothing at all. He drank and asked about the lady, but the cameraman shrugged: That's all he'd seen, or at least, he hadn't paid attention to her since there were other things to watch. He'd barely contained himself, it had been a struggle to keep the camera steady!

Sinking into the dream of memory, the friend emphatically gestured, drawing shapes in the air.—Blissful smiles; pure happiness.

"And then?" asked Pavlo; the dreamer awoke with a start. Well yes, then something had happened on the stage, as the armed crowds converged on the courtesans, but he hasn't seen that himself, his camera had been trained on the pit, in which - he'd forgotten to mention—an inhuman swell of bodies had trampled the duke; and then he asked again whether he, Pavlo, understood how a people, clearly not oppressed, and in the light of day no less, could take up arms, raise themselves from this state of non-oppression, and fly the banner of the king as though it were a banner of freedom: the student of history must explain this to him! Drawing nearer, the friend confided that he'd been ordered to deliver a statement to tomorrow's academic analysis, so his friend must offer him some assistance:

How would the Truly Truthful Sciences of History explain this bizarre event?

Annoyed, Pavlo tried to deflect, but his friend pushed another bottle of wine his way, so then Pavlo said casually, there was only one valid interpretation, the most valid that anyone could have, and for that reason it would remain a strictly internal matter. As the friend pushed a second bottle his way, Pavlo lowered his voice too, and with a distinct sense of impropriety he shared the conclusions of the SuCoC; the relieved cameraman exclaimed: That's it! Long gone and dark, that explains everything! And fully overcome, that was right! Then he left in a hurry leaving Pavlo behind, alone, drinking.

He drank, so that the lady might appear; he looked for her in the sea green of the coloured glass, but all he saw was the green of the synthetic bottle surrounding the synthetic substance W4, which he reluctantly, compulsively poured down his throat, until he fell asleep at the table. Even in sleep the lady did not appear to him; it was a dull, toxic twilight that was followed by nausea and fatigue in the morning; but as Pavlo had decided to skip the historical seminar - he'd falsely assumed his permission to audit had been withdrawn, perhaps he'd even been expelled from the university—he drank, eagerly, forcing down the nausea with the rest of the second bottle, before going to bed in broad daylight.

This time the lady appeared to him in his sleep, albeit only for a moment. He was standing in the pit, she approached. He saw her sea green and saw the scarlet of her bobbing poulaines come closer, weighted with promise, and he stretched up so he might see her face, hidden beyond his field of vision. As he humbly leaned towards the sea green seam, draped over the scarlet, the fabric parted before him and revealed the dwarf. Pavlo was horror-stricken. He wanted to swing his fist at the dwarf, but his arm moved as in slow-motion, and he wanted to shout: Go away! Go away! Only a whimper passed his lips. The dwarf stood with her legs spread wide, naked feet pointing outward, and Pavlo stared at her feet, terrified of the empty eye with neither lid nor eyebrow. He looked at her naked feet, splayed outward. The dwarf gathered her skirt. A green skirt, sallow green, like algae. Pavlo wanted to look away but couldn't. He saw the dwarf raise her skirt, the naked ankles, the naked calves, the naked knees, the naked hips, the pale, watery flesh padding the bulge of cartilage at the joint, and the dwarf pulled her skirt higher and higher and turned her feet and knees ever further outward. Pavlo, with insatiable repulsion, followed the incomprehensible spectacle, and now the dwarf bared, in her hairless lap, the empty hole of the pupil, a sucking eye swimming towards him, filling Pavlo with dread; the eye of the dwarf swam into his own, and in this moment Pavlo awoke.—Nausea; sweat; thirst; he stumbled to the sink, realizing to his dismay that it was the middle of the day. He swore he would never drink again for the rest of his life. Sickness rose from his stomach and he longed for a sip of schnapps. Since the room was spinning, he sat down and stared into the green of the empty bottle, contemplating ways to get more money, just to get through this nausea. And that's how it happened.

His friend helped him out one more time; he thought about the brilliant contribution he'd delivered at the academic analysis thanks to Pavlo's information and he showed his gratitude; Pavlo drank. - No lady this time, but no dwarf either.—Then Pavlo began borrowing money here and there, drinking schnapps instead of wine, then hooch instead of schnapps, and thus stooping ever lower, he racked his brain for any philosophical wisdom he might exploit for more money. That's how he suddenly discovered, in the synopsis of logistic symbols for implication and replication, an arrow pointing right and one pointing left, the symbol for holding together, and translating this insight into the realm of mechanics, he re-invented the safety pin, forgotten for a thousand years. He successfully applied for a patent, but once he discovered that the revenue stream would not flow his way but rather towards the presiding authority, namely the causality laboratory, he began developing his inventions on his own. He produced single items and sold them in secret.

As a replacement for the built-in insulators on the handles on cookware, which had been based on the principles of metamorphosis from hot to cold, but which never worked, he invented the oven mitt. But as soon as it became widely known, it was unscrupulously mass produced by rivals, which taught Pavlo that inventions, if they were to result in hard cash, would need to be sufficiently complex. So he invented a wearable snowflake sorter for meteorologists, he invented the 'smell specs', and a hair counting machine. He invented, solely for his own use, an automatic dream recorder, which didn't prove particularly useful, since he only had two distinct dreams now. In the first, he fell into one of the countless construction pits along his daily walk to the laboratory and cursed because nobody helped him out; in the second—but no, this dream is too painful; let's stop here.

Eventually, following the resolution he'd made in the lecture hall during the Ocular Demonstration, Pavlo invented a method which, albeit in the smallest possible way, allowed him to look a limited distance into the future; the method relied on the exploitation of anti-causality quotients, but that's another story.

He re-invented the brush (to glue carpets, since the pressure-method never stuck), the salt shaker, the tea cozy, the egg cup, and a boot that fastened by means of buttons (for walking on Uniterr's streets), and further developing the buttoning idea, he came close to reinventing the zipper (for the mistress of the captain of the capital city's monitoring troops, which would have left him set for life), but by then the hooch had taken its toll. His friends, especially the neutrinologist Jirro, called his condition "whalified", after the fabled prehistoric sea animal the whale, whose body, according to Uniterr's zoologists, consisted almost entirely of tears. Pavlo accepted the moniker. For a long time he wore it with honor, albeit also with hesitation. While he was working on the invention of the zipper, he gave up drinking for a few weeks. During these harrowing days of withdrawal, he remembered his old passion for the history of the middle ages, and reveling in the pleasure of clandestine books (to which he was granted access by clients waiting for zippers), Pavlo might have survived his abstinence, if not for Estienne Nouvielles's "Luciferian Chronicles" which he read for the first time as a text rather than an interpretation of a text, and which recalled for him the battle of Traulec in 1409; of Toul; and the duke; and the distant lady. A sudden revelation came to him, that the Truly Truthful Theory of History was completely correct: Toul had been victorious and the chronicler had hushed it up; the story had happened exactly as the Truly Truthful Theory of History had retroactively dictated it.

As Pavlo realized this, he was overcome with trepidation, dizziness and pride; he sat in his cubicle in a secret cell in the secret wing of the university library, monitored by cameras so that he would not make copies, or—matter forbid!—steal a page. He remembered requesting the SCIDIS and the distant echo of his “No!” as in a dream, and then he ran to the cafeteria, scraped together the last of his cash, and that was the beginning of the end for him.

Little by little, he forgot all about the duel and Jeanne Viole. His drinking continued; he did not escape, but he never invented another zipper. Strictly speaking - that is, in the sense of producing something—Pavlo never invented anything again; he merely dreamed of inventing. In his daydreams he invented the wildest things, and at night he dreamed his two dreams, usually the one with the construction pit, but sometimes the painful one; so we will describe it after all: Pavlo walks out to the edge of the sea and sees a jellyfish floating in the spray, staring at him like a lidless eye. He looks around to see if he's alone, and then he steps into the sea, to catch the jellyfish, and as he stretches out his hand –

But no; we'll stop here after all.

Consciousness Collection

When Janno, after a brilliant conclusion to his secondary education, applied for admission at the philosophy departments of Uniterr's universities, he was first of all assigned, in accordance with law no. 7, a time and date for the examination which it was absolutely essential to pass for any admission into higher studies, that is, to matriculate. This test not so much of knowledge as of disposition was officially called "statistical ascertainment regarding various selected parameters of the state of consciousness of certain population groups within the Truly Free State of Uniterr," or "Consciousness Collecting" for short," or, crudely, "The Mind Reading." For three weeks before the test Janno carefully washed his head, paying particular attention to his ears, which, jutting out as they did in baggy ridges, were especially prone to collecting dirt.

The state of his disposition was no reason for worry. He had always been the best in state consciousness class, and he knew that his homeland was the strongest and most powerful land in the world, unconquerable, untouchable, unreachable and for that very reason in particular need of a strong military defense. To be able at any time to counteract Libroterr's superiority with a defensive attack, and if necessary even annihilate it, which in a deeply historical sense was in fact in Libroterr's own interest, since the people there were forced into the oppressive slavery of unrestrained anarchy, quite unlike Uniterr, where, thanks to a healthily moderate standard of living and an order-ensuring shortage of those sources of dissatisfaction known as "personal rights," the people lived in secure contentment. Janno knew all that perfectly well, since this was the sum of what a citizen of Uniterr must know in order to be worthy of the nation's higher services.

Another sign of Janno's worthiness could be found in the fact that it never crossed his mind to ask a student who had already completed the ordeal for any details. It was clear to him that it was a secret procedure, and even a million pieces of advice would be no help to him. It would probably not be painful, and probably not particularly taxing for someone with a clean consciousness, and Janno did have a clean consciousness. And his daily head cleanings took care of the exterior, especially the ears. If he was only growing more and more anxious as the day of the test drew closer, that seemed only natural to him, or for the first two and a half weeks it did. Then came the trouble.

On the third day before the consciousness collection, in the twilight of memory between physical and mental waking, he was suddenly certain, lying there, that he would fail the test, and however much he pushed back against this feeling of certainty, there it stayed, the sort of nagging feeling that seems like it must portend the future just because it won't go away, a future that makes you shudder just to think about; a highly fatal condition, like the emergence of an illness, which, starting with slight inconveniences—sniffles, lightheadedness, a slight fever—still warns that these harmless seeming symptoms are the start of something more serious. A sniffle is easy to catch, and everyone knows how it feels to be sure you're going to fail a test; but it's a different kind of sniffle that leads to the flu, and it's a different kind of fear, not just run of the mill anxiety, that comes with the certainty that there must be a reason for it, even if that reason is impossible to know.

While Janno knew that the fear he was feeling must have a deeper cause, a melody came into his mind, one of those yearning tangos that never leave you: *black is your hair, your lips so red*. He would have taken this melody as a sign that he had overcome his fear through force of concentration, if he had not in fact taken it to mean that the fear came from a place he could not track. Nevertheless, he began to hum. This is the gallows humor of a not yet condemned poor sinner, who, unaware that he is going to the gallows, looks at the distant fluttering flight of the ravens as a thing of beauty, which both calms and terrifies him. Of course, these were not conscious thoughts, but rather took the form of otherwise unnoticed feelings, a bit more than a reflex, but not quite rising to the level of reflection. Janno was taken in and began to hum along, which was in fact a perfectly typical thing for him to do, but since he was having a crisis of confidence, it still struck him as an irksome disruption at the start of the working day.

He thought of how he might put a quick end to this uncomfortable situation, but as he tried to jump out of bed in one motion, he was hit by a pain in his stomach such as he had only ever felt after long nights on the town (of which he had incidentally had no more than five). He plopped back onto the bed, sat dully groaning for a moment, hoping that some cold water would refresh him, but couldn't quite seem to get himself back to normal. The nausea remained almost undiminished, but the melody had left his mind and the mysterious anxiety had also disappeared, and so Janno saw no reason to change his plans for the day, namely his usual walk, then re-studying the works of the comrade classics, and after that making lunch, and then after reading the classics once again, an evening visit to the cinema and an early bed.

Janno was hardly out of the house when, on the oval square surrounded by apartment buildings, he met a professor from the department he was applying for. They lived not only in the same building, but in fact on the same floor, and so they knew each other in the way that neighbors know each other: by face and name, maybe what the other did for a living, and each wrinkled his nose at the other's peculiarities: in the case of the professor, a faint odor of fish that seemed to always emanate from his clothes.

Wasn't he—what was his name again?—signed up for the consciousness collection on Friday, the professor, who happened to be a famous teleologist, the man who discovered the model for Uniterr's state structure in the structure of molecules, asked in response to Janno's greeting. Janno stammered out, "yes I am," and "Janno," (his identification number was visible on his jacket) and made an effort, in spite of the pain in his stomach, to smile and look the professor in the eye. The professor seemed to measure him up. Janno did not fail to notice that his answer must have seemed forced and his smile frosty; the nausea, briefly beaten back by the fresh air, was returning with full strength. The professor cleared his throat. Was he noticing that the applicant was afraid of the test? He hoped against hope to present himself to the professor as freely as his clean conscience called for, but he was doubling over in pain. On the dull concrete stood dirty puddles; in one of them a dead insect was swimming, grey in the reflected grey of the concrete, in which Janno saw his own face too.

The professor tapped him on the shoulder; the smell of fish; but it couldn't make Janno any sicker. Suddenly the thought came to him that this is what philosophy smells like, but this thought, or rather: the fact that he would think such a thing, did not repulse him; he took them both like his stomach pain, the feeling of complete helplessness, and suddenly the insane idea came to him, that his brain had a life of its own, an animal lodged in his skull, with its own breath, its own desires, all the brains of this city, of this nation, locked in bony walls, inaccessible, angry, unsatisfied.—A black flash. –The professor took his hand from Janno's shoulder—: did he have an idea what the candidate was thinking? His stomach muscles convulsed as he forced his neck to straighten, and as he looked into the professor's face, he saw behind the skull the professor's brain, that is, he thought he saw it, and it was a fish, and now he turned away, embarrassed.

"Well, as long as you're not afraid," said the professor. "If there's nothing to be afraid of, then there's nothing to be afraid of." Why did he say that? flashed through Janno's mind. He—what was his name again, Janno, right?—didn't have anything to be afraid of. Why did he ask that? "Yes!" Janno said, and now it was the professor who smiled, really smiled.

Janno looked back into the puddle, its face was as dismal as the concrete around it—the smell of fish; laughter; grey walls—The future studiosus, the professor explained, could not yet understand the double meaning of his "yes," depending on whether one took it as a response to the term "fear" or to the term "not." One could interpret his response as meaning that he did indeed have something to fear! –Janno saw that the sky too was concrete—Yes, yes, the concept of affirmation has its tricks, said the professor, laughing drily, it's the first thing you have to master, logic will teach the young *studiosus* that soon enough, assuming, of course, that it goes all right on Friday, but there's no reason to doubt that!—He walked toward the house, and Janno stood still; the professor had stepped in the puddle, and the dead insect flopped onto the concrete.—Janno's nausea became unbearable. He longed for a schnapps, but, upstanding young Uniterran that he was, he had no spirits at home, and it was too early to buy alcohol.

It was morning, high time for work; Janno stood alone at the bottom of the chasm between the looming colossuses, and it seemed to him that he was standing here for the first time, lost in an endless stranglehold; and suddenly, fully aware of what a ridiculous impulse he was following, but nevertheless driven by an inexplicable urge, he bent down, choked again by pain, to pick up the insect off the ground; but just as he was about to touch it, the troubling thought came to him that someone, maybe even the professor, could be watching him, and so Janno pretended to only be tying his shoe. He tugged on the knot and stole a quick look toward the door behind which the professor had disappeared; the entry panel, grey on grey, was closed. It was absurd to keep staring at it, it was made of one-way glass; you could only look out from the inside, and a two-way looking device was strictly prohibited on moral grounds; they were available only to the comrades in the People's Protection, and probably only high ranking ones. –Did they have a device for looking through solid walls?—For sure, and Janno immediately thought, why not? If you have nothing to hide, then you have nothing to hide. The insect lay on the edge of the puddle, a grey stripe with minute ridges, with six more tiny, barely noticeable streaks extending perpendicular; someone who hadn't seen it swimming in the puddle would hardly have been able to spot it. – Why did he bend down for it? It wasn't worth picking up; there were more than two dozen species of insect in the concrete biome, more than a dozen of which were threatened with extinction, but this was a perfectly common specimen. How long did he want to stay squatting here? What was he doing here, anyway?

Oh yes, a morning walk.

Oh yes, a schnapps.

While Janno struggled to straighten up again, he thought of the nearby restaurant where he was practically a regular; maybe he could talk to a waiter there; and hardly had this thought taken shape than his nausea receded, and in such a pleasant way that Janno didn't need the restaurant anymore. He was able to stand up straight again; the melody too returned, the one he had been humming when he woke up, and so he walked, without giving the insect another thought, almost at ease, along his route past the house fronts, entered his house, and could not help taking a look onto the square. It was empty; and Janno imagined someone, in the middle of the working day, was bending down to look at a dead insect, and he turned abruptly away.—The hallway was also empty. Janno didn't mind taking the stairs, since the elevation-transporter was still broken, the short way up to his floor, the twenty-second; he opened the door, automatically setting off the presence detection mechanism, and entered the private living cell granted to him in recognition of his studiousness (in general students lived in collective rooms), sat down at his work table under the fold-away cot, activated his reading device (number 4), which gave him the free choice of material, and devoted himself completely to his studies.

The morning flew by, and when the midday had also passed so productively, Janno, feeling accomplished at having synthesized seven important paragraphs of civics lessons with the words of the classics, decided to forego his usual lunch tin, since he had three consumption coupons left, to treat himself to a bite to eat in a restaurant, and headed out. He gave his destination and expected length of trip to the check-out device to activate the door, climbed down the twenty-two flights of stairs, and thought, as he stepped out of the house, that the professor he had seen in the morning could be the one performing his consciousness collection, and then immediately afterwards, in fact actually at the same time, that one can get used to the smell of fish, that it really isn't all that bad.

When Janno entered the restaurant, he heard the melody again, and caught sight of someone looking through the catalogue of the jukebox, and suddenly the feeling overcame him of having done all this once before: this pub; this jukebox; this person; him. –Janno had seen this a hundred times, and yet this time he felt something strange in the midst of the familiar, something deeply unsettling. Hardly had he taken his usual seat when the nausea returned; now he could drink a schnapps, but he was afraid to.—*Black is your hair, your lips so red* –: They were happy memories that these words awoke, the first crooning, the first notes, but nevertheless Janno staggered out in the mellow certainty that he would soon figure out the cause of his fears, and that this recognition would be his undoing.

And then a need to scream took hold of him.

Fresh air; the streets more alive now; the moving sidewalks were turned on; traffic lights shone through the gulleys; the People's Protector's with their people-catchers, and Janno dove into the crowd pouring out of the offices and businesses. Gradually he came back to himself, and the evening passed without further disruption. Janno ate in a restaurant, and for two consumption coupons that is, for two thousand fuel units, he also had a schnapps, went to the cinema, showered, slept passably well, awoke with no dark premonitions and without remembering any dreams and, with no morning walk, immediately set to his beloved work.

This time, however, it went slowly, and soon he was only marking time. He found it harder and harder to concentrate; where he should have remembered lines of doctrine, he instead remembered melodies, so hard were they to get out of his head that he couldn't help but notice how he kept unconsciously coming back to them. It was a battle of attrition against himself: In making the effort to concentrate, Janno felt that he was doing more to undo what he had already learned than to add anything to his memory. What was working against his will, what was thinking against his own thought? Had the comrade classics written about this phenomenon? But he knew perfectly well what was written there, it was quite clear and very simple: man is a thinking being, and his thinking is either right or wrong; if it is right, everything is fine, and if it is wrong, it can be corrected through instruction, as long as there is no conscious bad faith or the psychic anomaly of willful ignorance –: the first case fell under the auspices of justice, and the second was madness and belonged to psychiatry. He had learned all this; what could make him doubt it?—but he wasn't doubting it; he was only asking.—But was this question not already a doubt? If something is clear, there's no need to ask.—Janno felt like he was divided into two Jannos, only one of which could be correct, only which one was *he*, Janno, himself? Was he the right one, or was he the wrong one? But there could only be *one* thinking, thinking was bound to the brain, and Janno had only one brain, in only one head.—But what if inside his skull his brain was split in two?—Now Janno grabbed his head, feeling, with pointed fingers, and finally called himself to order. What nonsense, he was spinning, he hadn't slept well, it was all in his head, the remains of a strange dream, the after effect of the schnapps, after all he wasn't used to drinking! Enough, get to work!

Janno took an ice cold shower, persisting until the nozzle slipped out of his clammy hands, and began to soberly reconstruct what had actually happened.—Looking at it carefully, it was absurd: yesterday the dumb thought came to him that he would fail the test, that agitated him so much that he got a stomachache—yes, that was all, and then a melody popped into his head, and he couldn't get it out (incidentally: it was gone now!) and these two things, the stomachache and the jingle, had distracted him from studying. That was all, and it was nothing but nerves, and the best way to deal with nerves was quiet concentration.—Everything was fine, just fine.

He sat back down at his desk. *Black is your hair, your lips so red!* The melody rushed steadily up, and in a moment had overwhelmed Janno completely. He was no longer in any condition to take in a single one of the sentences there on the screen, sentences about the relationship between false and true, important sentences, correct sentences, which yesterday he could have recited in his sleep and which now, one letter after another, looked like some sort of imaginary creatures, and suddenly Janno thought, demoralized, that when they read his mind they would hear nothing but this refrain: *black is your hair, your lips so red.*—O matter, the mind reading was already tomorrow!—So then, you only have pop music in your head?—Was tomorrow Friday already?—Then today must be Thursday.—And he wants to go into upper service!—Was today Thursday? Then tomorrow was Friday!—Yes, today must be Thursday, since the mind reading was already tomorrow!—*Red is your hair, your lips so black*—Janno's thinking ran in circles, and so he didn't even notice that instead of "consciousness collection" he had used the slanderous (and obscene as well) expression "mind reading", a word from the vocabulary of agents, which he, as a future officer of the state, was obligated not to tolerate in his presence.

It could not go on like this.

Janno shut off the reading device, sat dumbly under his folded cot, felt the pressure in his stomach grow, and then it came to him that it would in fact be perfectly reasonable to ask someone who had just finished his mind—his consciousness collection, one of his comrade students, to offer some specific points of advice. But who? There were plenty of students in the building, it has been essentially constructed for the university, but Janno didn't know any of them well enough to ask for something so intimate.

What if he asked the professor?

Of course, that was it, the professor! Janno found nothing to object to in this idea. Why not the comrade professor? Had he not proven his good will, when he asked about the date of his examination, had he not with this question offered himself as a kind of mentor; had he not been waiting for the applicant to take him into his confidence? That was the only explanation for such insistent questioning, this offer was implicit in his question! And now Janno was already outside his apartment; and now he was already at the professor's door, but just as he was about to ring, when it occurred to him that part of the consciousness collection could be a test of whether he was approaching the coming examination with the equanimity of a clean conscience.

He decided not to ring on the bell after all, but his next thought was that when he left his apartment, he gave the residence of the professor as his destination. Even though they couldn't possible read through every routine entry, still, this one could be chosen at random.—Of course they would be looking carefully at his entries, he was an applicant for higher service, they have to take a good look at the candidates!—Janno had a wicked thought: he could say he rang and the professor did not answer.—But if the professor was waiting for his ring?—*Black is your hair, your lips so red*: the melody was back. And suddenly Janno heard the professor moving behind the door; he fled into the corridor; too late.

The smell of fish stepped out the door.

Will you look at that, the professor said, what a coincidence, that he should meet the *studiosus in spe*—what what your name again? Janno, yes?—Here, was he on his way to see him?

No, Janno stuttered, I mean: yes –

Was he perhaps looking for an explanation of his, the professor's, remark yesterday about the meaning of the term "term," and the antinomy of affirmation? "Yes!" said Janno and jumped back. Did this *yes* also have a double meaning?—Of course not; since: or, the professor continued, did the comrade candidate have any questions about tomorrow's consciousness collection: no, he did not!—did the professor see through him? He said: there was no reason for it, the consciousness collection was mostly for statistical purposes; he measured Janno up; and he smelled like fish.

Suddenly Janno saw the dead insect.

They went down the stairs together; the professor explained what was meant by "term:" Janno didn't understand a word of it. Did he understand, the professor asked, and Janno answered his "yes."

The square was in front of them, empty at midmorning; Janno did not know where the professor was heading; what did the professor know about him?—Where was Janno off to? asked the professor.—He stuttered something about a "morning stroll" and "review study;" he even managed a smile, and the professor nodded: "well, good luck again!" –He set of straight ahead and left Janno standing still.

Puddles on the concrete, there were always puddles, it was drizzling almost every day, and when it did stay dry, a cleaning truck dumped its dirty water.—Janno looked at the square, he had seen it a thousand times without ever seeing it quite like this: the grey colossuses of the apartment buildings, all of equal height, all of equal width, with even windows of the same size and the same shape and the same arrangement, the same doors and the same sills and the same alcoves under the same arcades; and the square poured out grey concrete; and the four oxygen sprinklers in the shape of a solitary tree: a trunk, six pipes as branches, the jets as fruit, and somewhere the dead insect.—The professor disappeared into the metro. Janno watched him go, the way you might watch a ghost fade away: did he also have to register his destination when he left his apartment?—Dumb question; of course he did, he was still a citizen of Uniterr, after all!—A dull thundering deep below the concrete: was the professor going to the university?—Dumb question: where else!—And suddenly Janno saw this square as a giant grey trap: only built up in order to come crashing down and crush someone beneath its wreckage: this concrete, these measurements, this wish to kill; and then all at once Janno was himself again.

How it happened to him is impossible to reconstruct. Maybe it was seeing the firmness of the concrete, this demonstration of secure self-solidity, which put an end to his confusion; perhaps his serious wish to concentrate on the test was finally coming true, a success at last, and not too late; maybe it was the professor's kindly calm demeanor; maybe all of the above; in any case, Janno was himself again. No disturbance, no fear, no stomach pain, and no oppressive, idiotic pop melody; and everything was obvious once again: that each apartment building was made of the same concrete as every other, that there were puddles on the concrete ground, a dead creature was swimming in one of the puddles, and once again Janno was in control of his time: he would go into the restaurant he had fled yesterday, and he would find the memory, with the clean consciousness of a clean conscience; there was nothing to be afraid of, and so he was not afraid.

A few minutes later, Janno walked into the restaurant.

He had no problem finding a seat at this early hour. He ordered his usual tea, which didn't require any consumption coupons, it came, since he was a regular, with an extra piece of sugar, he took a sip and went to the jukebox. A square box, painted concrete grey, a coin slot, five buttons, and this one: *Black is your hair*. Janno hated to see the coin go; he didn't really want to hear any music, and it didn't feel right to pay just to remember a song. But what could he do?—He turned on the machine; the waiter nodded contentedly; a guest said: "good!"—*Black is your hair, your lips so red*—: nothing; Janno heard the silly lyrics with their silly melody; no sign of memory, only what Janno already knew, so, no new memory: that, when he arrived in secondary school, he had eaten here with his parents, to celebrate his acceptance, that he had a meat dish, category III, and after that a chocolate dish, that a bottle of wine drink had stood on the table, that the jukebox was playing the whole time, and that someone kept interrupting the songs; but why? Oh yes, because his father had wanted it that way.—Nothing else?—Nothing else.—Janno finished up, paid, and went back to his apartment, studied, warmed up his lunch tin (he was saving his last consumption coupon for tomorrow), washed up, looked over what he had studied, had dinner, and as it grew dark he drew up a plan for tomorrow.

Friday—what would happen? Most likely, no, definitely, someone would attach electric wires to his temples, forehead, and the back of his hea—no, no, the beginning, how does it begin! Systematically, please: what exactly would happen?

He would walk into the university building, give his name to the guard, who would check his number and his admissions tag, he would go into the indicated room, and—wait, not so fast, there was already a problem: how should he behave, mentally, during this part? Think about something, or not? Of course think about something, but what? That the consciousness collection is right, and that I have full confidence in it: that's it! He would start the day with these thoughts, he would think them while he got out of bed, and he would keep thinking them until he stood in front of the guard.

Then he would walk into the room, only when they called him, of course, give a confident greeting, wait outside the door (or would there be others waiting? It didn't matter, he would sit with the others), then they would have him take a seat, attach some electrodes to his temples, forehead, and the back of his head, perhaps also insert monitors into his skull, there would be no pain, of course, probably no sensation at all, and he would, whatever happened, think about how this was for his own good, because it was for the good of Uniterr, and he was fully confident, and only Uniterr could have made such triumphs of science possible; and when that was done, he would think of Uniterr's mission, he had enough quotations from the comrade classics to choose from, to deepen this truth, to ground it historically, to explicate it with variations to account for present circumstances, this would surely go easily enough.—And under no circumstances must he forget to think something against Libroterr, say, that such a rotten society was completely incapable of achieving such scientific breakthroughs, since there they abuse the most sophisticated technical advances like consciousness collection technology, which in Uniterr served the common good, with their constant inhuman practices, rummaging around in the thoughts of their citizens.—Oh, that was a good thought, he mustn't forget that one! Think it just that way again, and again, and again; get it firmly in there.—That was probably enough. But for matter's sake, he mustn't think that he was thinking the right things, or let on that he was thinking for the test; it all had to seem natural; and it was natural; he did all of this out of his own free will.

More: if they asked him any questions, he would give short and direct answers, not impolitely, of course, not too curt, but also without being long-winded or sanctimonious, or trying to cram everything he knew into an answer, but that wasn't his style! If the procedure hurt, he would say "ow," openly and honestly, he wouldn't pretend, he wouldn't get caught up in contradictions. And if this melody did come back, what was that stupid line? Black is your hair . . . ?—But that would not be so bad; the youth of Uniterr is fortunate to be so well cared for, and to love life, which it is a pleasure to live, why shouldn't he show –; no, that was wrong, it should be: why shouldn't he *express* it?! What was this "it?" Why, his sheer happiness at having the good luck to be a citizen of Uniterr!—Of course: that circled back to Uniterr's mission, that was the pole star for his thoughts, and if he kept that always in mind, nothing bad would happen.

And besides, the consciousness collection was only for statistical purposes.

All right?

All right.—The night grew long.

Janno decided to take another walk.

He entered into the check-out device the code for "refreshing walk in the vicinity," (CC4) presumed duration "T/a2" (about an hour); the door opened; down the stairs; he stepped out of the house.

Stars and moon above Uniterr's capital.

The square lay deep in milky light, which sank heavily down from space and flowed imperceptibly over the concrete. There was a full moon, you could faintly hear the exhausters, which on the brightest night of each month sucked the dust from the streets of the city into the depths of the earth: a mighty subterranean rumble, the slow grinding of the pistons, echoed down after it, and in the blue emptiness of space, which filled the sky ever darker, the constellations followed the evening star and took their places in the sky. Janno didn't know any of them except the pole star; he watched how they shone from the firmament, over the vale at the bottom of the city where he stood looking up at them; underneath him the pumps hissed and hissed, and for a moment Janno could have believed that all this was happening just for him. There, where he stood, was the heart of space, and as the stars revealed themselves, it was as if the light's long journey had been bound for Janno's eyes all along.

At that moment there burst out, with a flash of energy that deprived the population of Uniterr's capital of power for a full hour, the message-bearing violet laser beams, shining out toward the shining stars, triumphantly wide, as tall as apartment buildings, messages from the most advanced part of the earth to intelligent beings on faraway worlds, and Janno's mind ranged out to them: he thought of how they rushed over immeasurable distances through the cold of space: what they would probably feel, when they received this message, signs in a universally intelligible language of signs, as the logicians of Uniterr guaranteed.—Did they probably look like humans, black hair, red mouth? Most people imagined them in the form of machines, robotic rumps, antenna organs, but Janno saw them looking like himself: beautiful like the humans of his planet, and free like the citizens of Uniterr.

Behind the square the violet flickering, beneath it the rushing sound, above it the expanse of space vaulting above the yellow moon.—The remains of the day had been sucked away, the clear light of night flowed around the houses; the puddles reflected the stars, and Janno suddenly had to cough: along with the dust, the warmth had disappeared, along with the celestial light, the cold breath of the heavens had come; no wonder that Janno was the only one in the square. The buildings in deep darkness; the exhausters fell silent; the silence of the night.—Janno tried to hold out for as long as the lasers were shooting through space, but the cold penetrated into his lungs, and so he went back inside.—Twenty-two flights of stairs; the elevation-transporter, although it had been repaired today, was stopped due to the power disruption; twenty-two flights of stairs, they warmed him right up.

Janno felt as though he were climbing to the stars.

Back in his living cell, Janno walked to the window; he knew that from this crack he could only see a fragment of one of the signs (here it was clear: the middle part of the left diagonal stroke of a column pointed upwards) which Uniterr was broadcasting into space;

and so he saw nothing behind the moon-yellow concrete except a distorted violet glowing, but this time he saw it in its full, truly cosmic significance, and it became all the more overwhelming to him: the flickering, Uniterr, outer space, the hour his life was taking him towards, it all only added to his confidence. Janno felt protected, and what he felt was gratitude.

Prepared, grateful, protected –: what was left for Janno to do except to go to sleep? Janno went to sleep and slept peacefully, four times he woke up, looked at the clock and went back to sleep, the third time, he remembered fragments of a dream: a robot-like being had stared into his face, and Janno had cried out.

And now it was Friday, a day like every other: alarm clock rings; turn off the alarm clock; yawning, sprawling between sleeping and waking; running water in the sink; running water in the shower; folding up his cot; breakfast tin; the morning speech from the radio, and while slowly chewing his carbohydrate tablet, Janno thought, as planned, that he had full confidence and that everything that would happen was for the good of Uniterr.

With these thoughts Janno walked into the university, and everything unfolded as he had expected: the guard in his booth; Janno gave his name; entered his identification number into the computer, as well as a fresh fingerprint and a body odor profile (taken by a miniature vacuum device, at ear height), and already the computer spat out a little metal tag, his admissions slip; the guard stuck it in the clock, at the exact minute of his appointment a green signal would appear above the door; the guard gave Janno the tag back, as well as a map with directions and a four-minute allowance; Janno stuck the tag to the lapel of his jacket; the door opens at the push of a button, and Janno at the exact second, walked into the interior of the house, which for the next five years would be his spiritual home, if . . .

I have, thought Janno, complete confidence, everything happens for the good of Uniterr!

The university, one of Uniterr's oldest buildings, was built in the decorative style from around the year 2000; it was known for its concrete ornaments around the pillars and the pierced tin frames around the oil portraits of the rectors, which lined the corridor of the administration wing, but Janno didn't notice them as he passed. He had no time, the four minute limit was strict. Down the hall; right around the corner; up two flights of stairs, the hallway on the left hand side, down one flight of stairs, once again to the left hand side, up two flight of stairs, the seventh door.—As he stood before it, a sign flashed: *No Entry—Wait!* Janno stayed where he was. The text dissolved, and in its place Janno's identification number appeared together with the instructions to put his admissions tag in the slot.—Janno did so; the door opened.—From the room came a woman's voice: "Come in!"—Janno went in; and the door closed behind him.

The woman's voice: "Sit down!"

The room was concrete, six bare surfaces; a chair; a table; a hatch window just below the ceiling; beneath it a three-legged stool; next to that a nail; hanging from that a hand towel; on the stool a plastic washing bowl.—Janno sat down. He looked for a cable, but saw none.

The waiting room, he thought, and then, immediately: I have full confidence! It is all done for the good of Uniterr. He waited for new instructions, but the voice did not return. Janno looked for where it had come from, but saw nothing but naked concrete. It was a dark voice, in a commanding, but not harsh, tone, endowed with a calm seriousness, it sounded like it was not coming from a recording, but from a living body.—Janno, the second time he heard it, felt a twitch in his brain, he imagined its owner, and he looked quickly at the concrete.—The hand towel was also grey.—I have, thought Janno, full confidence, it is all happening for the good of Uniterr; and he felt, silly as it seemed, like a machine, always thinking this same thought: did he have nothing else prepared? And suddenly an unspeakable word occurred to him, the most vulgar term for the female sex organ, and it came crashing into his well-prepared thinking like an enemy into a supposedly impregnable fortress: steadily, drumming, spreading paralysis wherever it went, and into the horror of his overwhelmed brain came another, even more unimaginable phrase.

Janno realized that his brain was thinking: *down with Uniterr!*

My god, there he was, about the take the test, Janno, not yet twenty years old, in his secondary school uniform, grey denim with grey buttons and on his epaulette the small violet star given to the top student in the school, and he is an enemy of his fatherland, the most advanced part of the earth, with which even outer space communicates. He sits there, as he was taught to sit, his bent forearms and open hands on his parallel thighs; his face is as grey as the concrete and we, who are telling this story, are not quite sure how to proceed: with a hypothetical explanation of how the unimaginable was able to come to pass (which would require both the passive voice of the pluperfect and future tenses), or with the usual simple past, presenting each thing in the order that it happened.—To continue with the latter course: although little could be said to have visibly transpired, nevertheless a great deal was taking place: Janno remained seated where he was, his mouth remained closed, as did his knees, his posture remained stiff, his gaze directly in front of him, only from his steadily widening eyes, whose clear whites were beginning to shine, could this leap of terror in this thoughts be seen in his body. For a second Janno sat perfectly still, then the whites of his eyes became dull, and his hands began to shake.

He was thinking comforting thoughts.—yes, he was –: he thought how fortunate he was that such an unimaginable thought had come to him before the test began, before they put the electrodes on his forehead and the back of his neck; that the enemy, who was hiding somewhere in his brain, had fired his shot too soon; and the relief that Janno felt, even if his body was still shaking, concealed the question of how the unthinkable had become in fact thinkable. He knew that he mustn't dwell on it, not with a thought, not with a feeling; already this knowing what was not permitted to be known was too much. Knowing what?—Nothing, nothing, nothing; it's over—I have full confidence, thought Janno, everything is happening for the good of Uniterr!

And he thought that he loved Uniterr, and it was not a lie.

There he sits, Janno, not yet twenty years old, black hair, red lips, concrete-grey face; he sits up straight in a stiff posture, and if all his nerves and pores are trembling, that is only from the shock of relief, for Janno does not know and cannot know, that this already *is* the test, and has been for some time: it began what he entered the room, and his examining committee—one of two hundred conducting a consciousness collection this morning, to whom two hundred applicants, all just like Janno, in identical rooms on identical chairs sitting in identical isolation, have been called—

already has his thoughts in front of them, is already decoding them. The three members of the committee are watching him through the one-way mirror behind the towel, studying his physiognomy. Of course it is the applicant's chair which captures the streams of his thought and transmits them, the signal strengthened by the elliptical, bowl-shaped receiver, and the mental processes in the applicant's brain appear as a coloured figure in space, at the same time that a computer captures them in written linguistic form.—Meanwhile the examiners read his physiognomy directly. So they interpret Janno's annoyed eye twitches as a sign of a memory (the figure in the bowl also suggests a memory, indicated by a particular colour, perhaps light blue), for Janno, however hard he resists, however much it is even possible to consciously keep a thought from entering one's mind, Janno suddenly remembers the story behind the jukebox in his restaurant, the grey box, the five buttons, the melody, and the drunken customer, who does nothing but stare at Janno with his empty face, and shouts into the open room, and Janno guesses what the man has shouted and he knows, and he tries not to hear it: at any moment the voice that called him into the room could return.

There is a clicking sound in the concrete.

Janno's heart misses a beat.

Silence; no call.—Did they forget about him?

But that's impossible.

Should he draw attention to himself? That would be impossible! And suddenly Janno felt his fear returning. A choking fear that he might vomit, and he sat, as he had knew how to sit; his stomach turned; he swallowed; it didn't help, and suddenly Janno thought, almost at a shout, that they couldn't do this to him, that they couldn't treat him this way, that he had the right to an explanation, that it is inhu—

and he threw up; and again the emptiness, and complete silence in the chamber; and Janno stared at the grey wall: the grey hand towel, the grey bowl, the stranger at the jukebox, the way he stood there and shouted and shouted and shouted –: no words, nothing but a shout, a groaning shout, stronger and stronger, the same cry that Janno was choking down; and then Janno thought that he had had enough, that he would get up and walk out, go demand an explanation, and as he pressed his hands against his thighs, the door opened and the professor entered. Is the candidate ill, he asked, still standing on the threshold; his tone sounded more like scolding than concern, and Janno, buckling down before his examiner, quickly shook his head no, and understood, as the professor—after a look almost of disgust, and not another word—stepped out and closed the door behind him, and the concrete again fell silent, that his test was well underway.

He heard the cry of the stranger howling and was certain that he was done for.

We do not wish to describe the two hours that Janno had yet to wait; let it suffice to report that they were the longest hours in Janno's young life. From the outside there was little to see: he sat there, after he had fallen back into his chair, choking on vomit, intermittently doubling over and even groaning when the urge overcame him, but nevertheless he fought to maintain his prescribed posture, his arms at right angles, his legs parallel to the legs of the chair, and he stayed in this position until the call rang out that he may come out now.—The interior matched the exterior: the movement of the cry, the struggle to suppress it, and the anxious attempt to keep his posture. The result was ultimately apathy.

This apathy was nothing but the logical conclusion of the initial paralysis. As Janno fell back onto his chair, and sunk for the eternity of a single second into utter thoughtlessness, the shock was the beginning of a recognition, of the recognition that he was done for, the paralysis and apathy that came with this recognition intermingled wonderfully.—He had just begun, and he already knew how it would end, and Janno looked upon it almost thankfully: finally, finally it's all over! The torture of waiting finally over, the ulcer of uncertainty burst, a therapeutic release of unbearable tension, and so Janno waited with certainty, and in this certainty almost eager (in which eagerness a plan was already taking shape of what he would do next, and so he also felt a breath of freedom) –: in this condition, Janno awaited the call that would cut him free of the university. But as time continued to stand still, grey and silent as the concrete, and no call, no explanation followed, Janno understood that he would not get off so easy, and that the comrade People's Protection would be called in, and he would be brought to where an enemy of Uniterr belonged! The thought didn't frighten him: prison, too, meant an end.—Nothing in Janno thought of fleeing.—The concrete remained silent; why was nothing happening? The comrade People's Protection must have arrived long ago: was the wait starting over again? And with the fear, Janno felt the cry rise up in him, and then, quite slowly, as he forced it down, like a slow opening-up of a full-petalled flower, Janno thought: it was his father's fault.

His father's fault, no one else's but his father's: why had he not covered Janno's ears when this reckless cry went out? Why had they even gone to that restaurant? His father must have known that such horrors happened there!—Where were the comrade People's Protection, so that he could confess everything to them; he would confess everything right away, they should know that he hated the enemy within himself, this stranger who had shouted his way into his brain, they have to give him the chance to make up for his thought failure, to prove his love for Uniterr –

It finally occurred to Janno that the only explanation for why he was still waiting was that they—stop: what liberties he was taking!—that the most respected comrade officers of the testing and consciousness collection committee were waiting for a statement from him, and that in that very moment he may have been wasting his final chance to come up with a quick conf –

("The C-D complex is coming rather late," remarked the professor in the examination chamber, as the model of Janno's thoughts took on the characteristic light yellow spirals)

—ession; and Janno wanted to jump out of his chair, when it occurred to him that he couldn't possibly leave now, he must think only about his confession, since the most respected lady and gentleman comrade officers of the consciousness collection committee could see directly into his brain. And as Janno was thinking this, the picture of his brain appeared to him, as they probably saw it, grey, puny, full of rot and decay, a repulsive, slimy, dirty mass, which he carried around inside his skull; he felt nauseated at himself, but no longer had the strength to contain his nausea; he still felt the wish, the dying hope, that the filth would be scrubbed out of his brain and his thoughts cleansed, just as they cleaned Uniterr's cities, with stiff brushes and strong bleach, but at the same time he thought that it would not be worth it, that he was too far gone for them to waste their time with someone like him, it was best just to forget all about him, and that this is just what would happen to him, and Janno felt his will depart from him, and his need to vomit passed away, all that remained was the dull waiting, already he felt nothing more than dullness, and as Janno didn't even perceive the passage of time, and had become just another part of the décor, there came ringing a voice, this time the professor's voice, announcing his identification number and telling him to stand up.

Janno stood up.

The door opened.

The instruction: step into the hallway.

Janno stepped into the hallway; a woman came out the next room carrying a canister of film in her hands, and walked past Janno. He did not watch her go.—The woman went down the corridor, the professor called out from the door; he did not look at Janno, who was looking straight ahead, and called the woman back, she had forgotten the B film.—The woman came back; Janno looked straight ahead; the woman, carrying one more canister, disappeared down the hall.

"B film," Janno heard, and he knew that what the woman was carrying off was the record of his consciousness collection, but his mind was empty of everything except the next command. "Now," said the professor from the doorway, "what was your name, Janno, is that is right?"—"Yes," said Janno.—No smell of fish.—"Now then," said the professor; a click in the concrete, and suddenly Janno once again saw the restaurant and the jukebox, and now he saw without hearing, but in unmanageably slow motion, how the waiter rushed over to the machine and turned the volume up to an earsplitting level over the sound of the stranger's shouts: *black is your hair, your lips so red.*—The sound was enough to split Janno open.—"Come with me," said the professor.—No People's Protection?—Janno entered the other room.

A round table, two unfamiliar faces; the professor sat down; Janno lingered at the door.—The three men looked at him.—No instructions.—My confession! thought Janno; they are waiting for my confession! But he spoke not a word. The three looked at him, and Janno wished that they could still see inside him, to see how he was trying to confess; could they see it in his eyes? Or in the cry that was rising up in him again?—"I," he began; and the choking sensation returned; he concentrated on the tips of his shoes.—They were filthy.—The scraping of a chair; a crackling sound; the professor picked up three rolls of film that were lying on the table in front of him. My brain in your hand, though Janno, and he was almost amazed: You have my brain in your hand! He stared at the dull shining grey of the plastic case around the three rolls, and suddenly he saw through them, and saw the dead insect floating in the dull, sloshing water, and the insect lifted its head and gave him a disconsolate look. Janno couldn't take it anymore; he closed his eyes when he heard the professor speaking again: The consciousness collection, the professor was saying, had been the cause of unprecedented slander from Uniterr's enemies, a dirty, a filthy, a stinking provocation –

("dirty," and "filthy" and "stinking," Janno heard these words and knew where they were coming from)

a dirty, a filthy, a stinking provocation, propagated by dirty, filthy, stinking brains, he would not help these lies along; suffice it to say that this, the consciousness collection, was for statistical purposes only; therefore he wished to ask number (and here followed Janno's identification number) officially, whether he gave his permission for these recordings to be used for statistical purposes; if he did not give his permission, they would, naturally, be destroyed on the spot.

Janno heard the words; his eyes were still closed, and he saw the woman whom he had not watched walking down the corridor with his tapes; the door opened, the woman came back.—Janno saw her: empty hands.—"Well?" asked the professor; "yes!" said Janno; and over the muttering sounds of the others beginning to speak, the professor said: there it is again, the ambivalence of affirmation (and he explained to his colleagues that this remark was in reference to a recent conversation he had had with the candidate); and to Janno: it is once again unclear whether his "yes!"

referred to the use of the recordings, or to their destruction. —"Yes!" said Janno.—The woman laughed; the muttering grew louder; one of the examiners struck the table. A conciliatory gesture from the professor: it is understandable that (Janno's identification number) should be having difficulty pulling himself together, so he would ask directly: how did he (identification number) consider the state of his own consciousness?

The insect in the concrete; now it was too late.—The confession –; Janno staggered; he looked for support from the wall behind him; he leaned the back of his head against it. For all this time, he had had the chance to voluntarily confess, all this unimaginably long time, but now it was finally over!—It was completely inappropriate to be leaning on the wall, before one's superiors one should stand free and upright, they had practiced that way back in elementary school.—"Do you have a hearing problem?" asked one of the examiners.—The woman laughed.—The dirty shoes.—"I," Janno swallowed, "I am a –" oh, the scream, the scream!—Was he screaming at him? He didn't know.—"At least stand up properly," said the other examiner, "surely that's not too much to ask!"—"Yes!" said Janno and pushed himself away from the wall; he swayed, but stayed standing.—"I am—I am a stinking—stinking—"he shouted, and he shouted in a violet buzz: *black is your hair*; someone took hold of him.—"Give him a glass of water," Janno heard the professor say, or was it the loudspeaker, he didn't know; he felt that he was sitting on a chair, concrete, a backrest, hard, hard legs, milky circles swirled around him; he felt a glass of water; he drank.—"I believe that much is clear," said someone. "Yes," said the other.—The smell of fish.

The professor stood before him.—Now, he said, the name was Janno, right?—and now shockingly close: It remained of the utmost seriousness, what had emerged in the thoughts of comrade Jan-

("comrade" sounded disbelieving to Janno, "comrade—*comrade*—COMRADE")

-no, simply unbelievable what was piled up in there, more unbelievable yet was the lack of guidance in Janno's life up to this point, and the comrade candidate will himself have come to the conclusion—at least it appears that way—that it is quite necessary to decline his, one might well say, audacious application; only –

(silence, and shining, divine radiance, and Janno stood up from the chair, staggered again, and stood, stood free, stood upright)

only it belonged to Uniterr's basic law to believe in the good in people, especially in such a young person, who after all showed good will in so vigorously seeking to understand himself and—this he wished to underscore—in steadfast devotion to the future guidance of his comrade teacher to eradicate entirely the enemy within; he was granted the opportunity to make use of a probationary period with full effect –

And Janno, flooded with painful happiness, could hardly believe what he was hearing and knew that he would never be able to thank his fatherland sufficiently for this magnanimity of Uniterr: in spite of all the filth in his brain, his comrades did not let him fall, they offered him their hand once more, gave him another chance, and he heard his professor speak and felt tears in his eyes and through the tears he saw his helpers sitting in front of him, they who wished only what was best for him, and if they had been a bit rough with him, they had only done so for his own good, and when the professor asked once again whether the candidate agreed that the recordings of his consciousness collection be used for statistical purposes, Janno gave an emphatic "yes!"

The professor nodded; the others nodded; Janno nodded; the woman smiled.—On the table the rolls, in dull grey packaging, in the mild light of the sun, beautiful. What a worthy end: noble, helpful, and good.—It was therefore his task, the professor said, to share with the citizen Janno that his request for permission to study had been conditionally accepted: with a period of probation, the terms of which would call for a cleaning of his consciousness, and in this cleaning of consciousness and of thinking, a fellow student would or other citizen would make a substantial contribution –: does he accept this decision as his own?

And while Janno, entering into the higher service, delighted and ashamed of the completely undeserved mercy, softly but firmly repeated his "yes!" he was thinking, and at the same hour thousands of others in this building, and hundreds of thousands of others in identical buildings were also thinking, that the words "consciousness collection" contained more than merely statistical meaning: it is truly a gathering up of consciousness and an elevation into the airy heights of true purity.

Janno, glowing in this recognition, considered for a moment whether he would dare share this insight with his comrade teachers, perhaps as the first proof of his purifying introspection; at that moment the professor somewhat impatiently said, "that's it, then!" –

And Janno, understanding that he had already taking up too much of their valuable time, greeted his educators the way he had been practicing since elementary school, looking them straight in the eye, holding his body perfectly upright, his body, which at this moment was fully at one with its spirit; and while the woman filled out Janno's admissions sl—

But all that is of no real importance. Of course he took his consumption coupon into his restaurant that evening; and of course the melody came from the machine; and of course he later went on to sleep with the professor's secretary. One of his first probationary tasks dealt with his father. But that is really not very interesting.

Pavlo's Paper Book

It is simply untrue that paper books are forbidden in Uniterr. On the contrary: they're safely stored with all imaginable care in special libraries where they are made available to scholars. Yes, even private individuals are allowed to own and read paper books; they can even borrow them. The only thing that is forbidden—due to the historical and cultural value of these priceless materials—is the debasement of these books to a commodity. No objections can be made to that kind of protection, and obviously—as per Uniterr's constitution and mission—any paper books containing destructive, immoral, that is to say hostile to Uniterr, or otherwise harmful or possibly harmful content, have been sequestered and made accessible only to a strictly limited group of people.

After Uniterr's two nuclear wars, the human realm contained the respectable number of 82,347 fully preserved Category I paper books, and the number of Category II books was estimated at 1.2 million.—The term 'paper book' was understood to include "any type of print product of vegetable or animal origin, which can be consumed without the use of a mechanical medium (reading device, film, audio equipment, etc., excluding eyeglasses or a basic magnifying glass)".—Category 2 paper books were items of demonstrably less historical or material value: blank mass-produced forms, a torn-out calendar page, a book sleeve, an envelope; a written postcard on the other hand could, depending on interpretation, belong to Category I. Among its first measures, Uniterr's government had confiscated all paper books located in private collections for the purpose of inspection and registration. The illegal sale of privately owned books was duly punished, typically by loss of body. After registration had been completed, the majority of copies were allocated to libraries as national treasures, though in a total of thirty-one cases, some paper books of this type were returned to their owner,. Category II paper books had to be declared as well; and in particular, the method and means of acquisition had to be established in detail. These were prized collector's items; for example, nothing made Jirro's father as proud as his sales receipt from the year 1998, for the purchase of a piece of soap substitute (for 49.99 marks) from Superstore 22 in a city by the name of Berlin, which was destroyed in the first nuclear war. This piece, unique in its own way, hung framed in a protective krypton glass case on the front wall of the family living cell, where it gave Jirro's father the opportunity to embark on deep philosophical contemplation about human progress, whenever guests visited. Back in these distant, dark times, he explained, people were still forced to purchase soap substitute in stores, whereas Uniterr's government, always putting the wellbeing of its people first, distributed a piece of soap substitute at no cost on a monthly basis, for which they should be eternally grateful.—Nodding, marveling, murmurs of admiration—and then a visitor would inevitably exclaim: "One thousand four hundred and eighty five years ago . . . incredible!"

And then all would nod again.

Now it just so happened that Pavlo got his hands on a Category I paper book, and namely one of the 31 that were held in private collections. The exact circumstances are unimportant; let it suffice to remind you that Pavlo used to work on inventions at the behest of a comrade leader of the Capitol Patrol. He still enjoyed the patronage of this comrade, who then arranged the loan of this book to Pavlo from among her acquaintances. However, it's important to point out that paper books are fundamentally different from records on microfilm or reading cards[1], typically dating to the

---

[1] That's aside from the so-called extract of contents for cultural knowledge repositories (for example: "Macbeth. Blank verse play in five acts by W. Shakespeare [1564-1616], deals with the sweeping away of an unjust tyrant by a militia army"—as it was recorded in Uniterr; in Libroterr, this extract read: "MacBeth.

interbellum between the first and second atomic war, which was how a considerable amount of world literature from the Epic of Gilgamesh to Dante, and from Beckett to Smith, Schmidt, and Szmyd had been preserved in text. The definition of a paper book, we repeat, included its ability to be consumed without mechanical mediation, or, to be concrete: Pavlo understood what a paper book was, since he was holding one in his hands.

It could be touched like a human body! He caressed the blueish grey, supple binding. The book lay in his hands like an animate object. He opened it, one could open it! His hand sensed its resistance and surrender, the writing appeared in neatly ordered blocks, visible but not yet decipherable. The pages curved like hills, in the center a valley of shadows—shadows from Pavlo's finger as well - he could sense the contours as it slid across the lines of symbols. The letters smelled like darkness and distance, one could hear the leaves rustle as they flowed, an inexhaustible source of time slipping away.—He had not yet started reading. He just took it in, and did so with all of his senses.—Neither microfilm nor reading disks were self-revealing objects that could be sensed physically outside of the machine. Microfilm consisted of a tiny

---

Play in five acts by Shakespeare, William [1564-1616]; allocable to the Gamma-II-ZP[2a] structure of the tragi-conflictory conjunction of three unresolved Oedipal complexes (fmm) within archaeo-feudal sociomicrostructures.)

little tube, indistinguishable in the hand from laxatives or diuretics; the reading disks were somewhat tangible, at least the outdated ones—a thumbnail sized piece of plastic. However, usually they were pre-integrated into the machine, retrievable by touchpad, like most computers: that's how you turned on washing or voting machines, calculators, alarm clocks, and living cell finders as well. The text, which would then appear, was a standardized figure composed of roster points like all information transmissions: intangible, inaudible, scentless, flavorless, and in no natural proportion to a human organ—least of all to the human eye.

The paper book was, first of all, simply convenient; it lay in his hand (and we say this on behalf of Pavlo, who searched in vain for a comparison) like a bird in its nest, and each of its pages was an image that could be delineated with the human eye, a wealth of space, self-contained, and thus also a measure for time. This measure was human, yet straightforward; one could use it to plan and resolve to read only two more pages, or three, or seven, or a hundred. On a reading screen or under the magnifier, the text scrolled by with no apparent end, though its speed could be controlled and you could pause it whenever you felt like it, yet the text, once paused, would look like a diffuse string of words, amorphous, lacking perspective, a random excerpt, in which often not so much as a sentence appeared. Where a paper book created mental space, a reading device became a conveyer belt lurching from one location to another; and even though the user could guide this belt along its entire length, it was never comprehensible anyway. In the best case scenario, the text was a quote. A microfilm tube provided no sensory way to determine how much reading time remained. A paper book could be weighed by the hand and by the eye, you could see it when it was in front of you, and as though it were introducing itself, its name appeared on the spine as a title, in this case: *In Dire Straits*. It dated from the same year as the cash register receipt owned by Jirro's father and it comprised, in not yet anglicized German, three texts characterized as "stories"; Pavlo had never heard of these stories nor their authors.

The first story was called "In the Penal Colony" and it began as follows: "It's a peculiar apparatus," said the officer to the traveler, gazing with admiration at the device, which he knew well of course. It seemed the traveler had only responded to the commander's invitation out of politeness, after being invited to attend the execution of a soldier condemned for disobeying and insulting his superior. Of course, interest in the execution was not very high, not even within the penal colony. At least, here in the small, deep, sandy valley, surrounded by barren slopes, the only people present, apart from the officer and the traveler, were the condemned man, a vacant-looking man with a wide mouth and unkempt hair and face, and the soldier, who held the heavy chain to which the small chains were attached, binding the Condemned Man by his feet and wrist bones, as well as by his neck, and which were also linked to each other by connecting chains. The Condemned Man had an expression of such dog-like resignation that he looked as though you could set him free to roam around the slopes and would only have to whistle at the start of the execution for him to return."

Pavlo read; and though he was at a loss for meaning when it came to many words (for example, he didn't know what a penal colony was), the text began to make more sense with each word, since, even though everything he read in it seemed unthinkable (for example that a soldier could disobey), and entirely unimaginable as having really happened, he read it as though he were spellbound, as though someone were telling him a story that was happening to him, Pavlo, though he only just now realized it.—"He sat on the edge of the pit, into which he cast a fleeting glance."—Pavlo had never sat on the edge of a pit, yet suddenly he could sense the abyss pulling him down.—Was the bloody water already rushing past him, trickling down into a stream of vomit below?

As the story continued, the officer was attempting to explain the execution device and along with it the essence of the penal colony, an ideal of discipline and order which had been drained by reforms, in an attempt to win the foreign visitor over to his party, the preservers of the old order. Pavlo saw the device in the wan gloom of the sandy valley and he saw it between the curving slopes of the book, which he held in his hands. He stood there, black against yellow sand, an enormous erect insect in his tripartite body, below him the bed, onto which the guilty person is strapped with a felt stub stuffed in his mouth and—after having comprehended his punishment—a bowl of rice for his last supper. Above, hanging from a band of steel, was the glass harrow which engraved the law onto the body of the condemned man with a thousand needles, for twelve hours straight, ending with the fatal piercing of the forehead with a steel spike. The inscriber hung in a trunk suspended above the bed, guiding the oscillations of the harrow, a highly artful system of gears, devised and created by the brilliant mind of a man who had once been the founder of the penal colony, and who remained the head of the officer's party even after his death. Pavlo could see him adjusting the inscriber; which dirtied his hands. The officer washed them in the dirty water, and as the water proved too dirty, in the sand. The condemned man and his guard watched; and Pavlo watched them, how they watched, he saw all of them through the glass harrow, and he recognized none of their faces though he knew them all. "Then I had the man put in chains. Very easy." None of Pavlo's acquaintances had worn chains (Pavlo didn't know anyone who had worn chains).—The soldier scribbled in the sand, bored; the condemned man, with dumb curiosity, pulled him closer to the machine.—He doesn't even know he's been tried and condemned, thought Pavlo, who had already read it in the paper book, and now it would be written on his body.—The condemned man was strapped to the bed and prepared; the book felt heavy in Pavlo's hands; the condemned man vomited.—The officer was disgusted.—How could anyone put this felt gag into their mouths without revulsion, when more than a hundred men had sucked and bitten it in the throes of death? Pavlo could feel it suffocating him.—"This is all the Commander's fault!" cried the Officer as he desperately rattled the brass rods at the front, "My machine's filthy as a pigsty." Hands trembling, he showed the Traveler what had happened. "Didn't I just spend hours making the Commander understand that prisoners should not be given food on the day before their execution? But this new, lenient regime has different ideas. The Commander's ladies like to cram sugary treats down the man's throat before he's hauled away. His entire life he's been feeding on stinking fish, and now he has to eat sweets! But that would be fine —I'd have no objections—but why don't they get the new felts I've been asking him about for the past three months?"

How might this end? thought Pavlo; the Officer appeared to be in the right, yet that seemed unbearable to him at this moment.—The Officer had developed a plan, to bring the new commander back to the spirit of the old ways, with the help of the Traveler. The Traveler just needed to help. It was a unique situation, but after a moment of hesitation, the Traveler refused.—There's a third man, thought Pavlo; the realization struck him like black lighting.—""So you're not convinced by the procedure," asked the Officer; "No!" cried Pavlo.—The Traveler remained silent.—The Soldier crouched before the bed in the sand and made friends with the condemned man, and that's when Pavlo knew how the story must end: The Traveler and the Soldier overpower the Officer, free the Condemned Man, and together they eke out an existence in freedom.—Pavlo trembled; it was terrifying.—In his distraction he had lost his place in the book; eagerly he looked for the continuation; the shadows of his sliding hand. - ""So you're not convinced by the procedure," he said"—that's the Officer, thought Pavlo—"smiling the way an old man smiles at the silliness of a child, concealing his true thoughts behind that smile.

"Well then, it's time," he said at last and suddenly looked at the Traveler with bright eyes that intimated some sort of demand, some kind of call for participation.

"Time for what?" asked the Traveler uneasily, but he received no answer.

"You are free," the Officer told the Condemned Man in his own language. At first the man didn't believe him."—Pavlo believed it—he understood everything now: This sudden mercy was a ruse by the Officer, to quash the pact between the three, since now, Pavlo realized, the traveler was being strapped into the machine.

""Pull him out," the Officer ordered the Soldier." He obeyed; the tension! Though he knew the ending, how would they get to it?—The condemned man had been freed; the Officer—what baseness!—showed the traveler a different pattern to guide the harrow's new needle path. The Traveler however could not decipher the script which was meant for him.—"Then the Officer began to spell out the inscription and then read them all together once more. "'Be just!' it states," he said. "Now you can read it.""—What was that supposed to mean: *be just*? thought Pavlo, surely that made no sense here!—"The Traveler bent so low over the paper that the Officer, afraid that he might touch it, moved it further away. The Traveler said nothing more, but it was clear that he was still unable to read anything. "'Be just!' it says," the Officer remarked once again. "Could be," said the Traveler. "I do believe that's what it says." "Good," said the Officer, at least partially satisfied. He climbed up the ladder, holding the paper. With great care he embedded the page in the inscriber and appeared to fully rotate the gear mechanism."

Now he's going to lay the Traveler underneath, thought Pavlo, and he would turn to the freed man with a fiery, rousing speech, and they would overpower the Officer—and Pavlo's thoughts were hijacked by a desire for the three to strap the Officer into the machine next, though he didn't think it through to the end, it was too grotesque! The verdict would fit but how could the officer have come up with that; it was surely an oversight on the part of the author. And only then, while the Soldier and the freed man mindlessly killed time, as the Officer took off his uniform and laid himself beneath the harrow, naked and disarmed, and put the felt into his mouth, did Pavlo realize nothing made sense to him anymore. He felt cheated out of his ending, and there was no more excitement about how this story might come to an end.—A ludicrous flight of fancy!—Yet Pavlo couldn't stop reading. Suddenly, the Officer was impaled by all of the needles and the steel spike at once, pivoting over the waste pit, as the machine inaudibly committed suicide (what else could you call the machine's expulsion of all of its gears from the inscriber?). Pavlo wanted to stop reading, yet he saw that only two pages remained, and resolved to read through to the end. His disorientation turned to helplessness.—Whereas he could now parse such previously incomprehensible terms as "penal colony", "leather folder", and "embellishment", even if he couldn't pin down their exact definition, and there were no unrecognizable words at this point, the unfathomable ending still rendered the entire story incomprehensible. Everything disintegrated, like the gearwork of the inscriber. It simply ended: instantly, illegitimately. After the punctured corpse of the Officer had been dumped into the pit (at least, that's what Pavlo thought he read), the Traveler, and with him the Soldier and the Convict, went into the city and disappeared into a 'tea house'. There, the Traveler learned that the old Commander had been buried under one of the tables, where some guests ("presumably dockworkers") had been sitting until the strangers walked in. Following along with the Traveler, Pavlo read the inscription on the gravestone: ""Here rests the old Commander. His followers, who are no longer permitted to carry names, buried him in this grave and erected this stone. A prophecy holds that the Commander will rise again after a fixed number of years. From this house he will lead his followers to recapture the colony. Have faith and wait!""—And then? Then nothing at all. The Traveler left; the other two stayed behind; the Traveler went to the harbor, but the other two soon followed; the Traveler jumped into a boat, and the sailor cast off from the shore at once. They could have still jumped into the boat, but the Traveler picked up a heavy, knotted rope from the bottom of the boat, threatened them with it, and thus prevented them from jumping."

But what kind of an ending was that! Where was the explanation of who was good and who was bad? Who was right and who was wrong? Whom we should emulate and whom to unmask? Where was the conclusion, what had been proven, rectified, refuted? In the end, the reader didn't even know who exactly this traveler, who had shown up at the island, had been, and now he was already sailing back home. Surely that couldn't be the ending! Yet not a page had been torn from the book, the pages were numbered consistently; this ending happened on page twenty-one, and on page twenty-two a new story began. Pavlo felt crushed: He'd begun the story full of hope, even though it was grim from the beginning. Yes, even the shudder of grimness created a sense of hope for a happy ending, and that ending was still so close, just within reach. The successful flight from the penal colony would have set an example for all, and now, as if it was mocking him, the next story was called, of all things, "The Torture of Hope".

So what was that about?

Pavlo read the name of the author: Villiers de l'Isle-Adam. A strange name. An impossible name. That's what people were called in the olden days, though owing to his study of history, Pavlo could actually pronounce the name correctly: Villyay de Leel Ahdam.

The story was set during the days of the Inquisition, and Pavlo was suddenly transformed into an old Jew (he didn't know what that was, but that's what he was); his name was Rabbi Aser Abarbanel and he was imprisoned in Saragossa. He discovered that he was to be burned at the stake in the morning; the Grand Inquisitor of Spain, the honorable Pedro Arbuez d'Espila, had personally appeared before him to announce the news: "My son, rejoice: your trials here below are coming to an end. Even in the face of such obstinacy, I must give permission for the use of such severe measures, though I do so begrudgingly. Still, my brotherly task of correction has its limits. You are the restive fig tree which, so often found without fruit, is condemned to wither away. God alone can judge your soul. Perhaps the light of eternal mercy will shine on you at the supreme moment. We must hope! There are examples . . . Amen! Rest in peace this night. Tomorrow you will participate in an auto da fé, that is to say, you will be delivered to the quemadero, the premonitory fire of the eternal flame: It only burns at a distance, you know, my son, and death requires at least two if not three hours before it arrives, thanks to the protective cloths, dipped in ice water, which we wrap around the head and heart of our offering with great care. You will only live to be forty-three. Consider that, being last in line, you will have enough time to invoke the Holy Spirit and offer him this baptism in fire which comes from God. So place your hope in the eternal light and sleep."

Thus spoke the honorable father grand inquisitor, and then he left his cell, after which, like his companion, the honorable brother torture master, he humbly asked the prisoner for forgiveness for all they had been forced to do to him. Now as Pavlo sat in his cell, in the darkness of night and in the knowledge of tomorrow's fiery death, he sank into a fever dream of hope only to discover that his dream wasn't a dream at all: The door had not clicked into its lock, the road to freedom lay open before him.—Oh what a shock, oh faltering heart!—A musty scent, the scent of moss: there was no doubt about it!—Quietly, quietly Pavlo pushed the door open and dared to look outside: "In the safety of a wan darkness, he discerned, first of all, a semicircle of earthen walls within which were embedded spiral steps; and above them, five or six stone steps high, a kind of black archway, which led into a vast corridor. He peered up and could only glimpse the first few arches from where he was."

Pavlo lowered himself onto the floor and crawled up to the edge of the threshold: The corridor seemed endless, yet it was a path to freedom! A pale light, the bluish moonlight, clouds drifting by. Not a single door was visible along the entire length of the hallway, but Pavlo knew: He was saved! He would make it! And even when—he finally understood the title!—And even as this dangerous hope for a road to freedom tortured him to down to his nerve endings, he knew he would make it, he must.

Having taken a step towards freedom, how would he ultimately get away?—Pavlo, entranced by the book, didn't give much thought to his own obsession with the word freedom, he barely noticed it. Eagerly, his eyes slid across the lines; eagerly, he slid along the floor, and it happened as he had expected: he would be tested down to his nerve endings; it was the torture of hope, and he persevered. Monks stepped out of the darkness, he pressed himself into the alcoves of the wall, dreading the sound of his beating heart, fearing the glistening sweat on his brow, and yet he knew that he would succeed. Flat, nothing but a shadow across the ground, he slid further, again becoming one with the wall when, above him, he heard two inquisitors dwelling on a theological dispute. Suddenly, "one of them, listening to his interlocutor, appeared to lock his eyes on the rabbi! And under this look, a distracted expression he couldn't quite figure out, the unfortunate man thought he could sense hot tongs once again biting his poor flesh; and once again he became a singular lament, a singular wound. Helpless, no longer able to breathe and with trembling eyelids, he shivered as the robe grazed him. How unusual, and yet how natural: The eyes of the inquisitor were clearly those of a man preoccupied with the response he was crafting in his head; a man who was fully and completely absorbed in thoughts about what he was listening to. His eyes were pointing forward—and seemed to look at the Jew without seeing him.

And indeed, after a few minutes the sinister pair slowly walked away. Still speaking in hushed voices, they made their way in the direction of the archway from which the prisoner had come: they didn't see him!"—Onwards, onwards!—Frightful apparitions everywhere, shadows of monks playing tricks on him across the walls, onwards, onwards, line after line, Pavlo slid along to the end of the page, and there he was, at the end of the hallway in front of a heavy door. He felt along it: no latch, no lock; then: a handle! The handle gave way below his thumb: Quietly the door opened before him.

The blueish night, its wafting scents, the tortured man gazing out into freedom. Taking a breath in safety, the thought suddenly came to Pavlo that it could be no coincidence that this story followed the absurd first one by—what was the author called again? Oh right: Kafka. This story corrected the previous one with a real, proper ending, and this ending also corrected the speech by the Grand Inquisitor, who had promised a rescue through the torture of flames in the afterlife of Heaven. No, the escape lay here on this Earth, through the torture of hope into freedom; that's how the road went, and now it had finally ended: a shimmering garden lay before him! Ecstatic, Pavlo looked back at the book: the blueish night in his cell, the moon framed by the window and the drifting clouds, and the scent of the open night! Pavlo didn't want to continue reading.

Everything had already culminated in a happy ending; was it not too much for him to demand confirmation?

He was filled with ecstasy. "He was filled with ecstasy." - Pavlo read this sentence, just one more, for closure, and then it seemed to him as though he saw the shadow of his arms appear across the page of the paper book, and he read: "Then it seemed to him as though he saw the shadow of his arms come at him: It was as though he could feel these shadow arms clasp him, wrap around him, and now he was softly pressed against a chest. Indeed, there stood a tall figure next to him. Confidently, he rested his eyes on the figure. And then he stood there, gasping, as if he'd gone crazy, with murky eyes, his entire body trembling, swollen cheeks, foaming at the mouth.

What a shock! He found himself in the arms of the Grand Inquisitor himself, the Honorable Pedro Arbuez d'Espila, who was looking at him, eyes filled with heavy tears and the look of a good shepherd reunited with his lost sheep.

The somber priest pressed the unlucky Jew to this heart with such fervent charity that his coarse, monastic hair shirt chafed the chest of the Dominican under his habit. And it began to dawn on Rabbi Aser Abarbanel, whose eyes bulged beneath his eyelids, choked with anguish in the arms of the ascetic Dom Arbuez, that all phases of this fateful evening had only been a calculated torture: hope. The Grand Inquisitor, with a look of concern and in a tone of poignant reproach, whispered in his ear with a burning breath made foul by fasting: "Oh my child! Would you abandon us on the eve of your potential salvation . . . !"

The paper book: Pavlo held the book in his hand; he held it closed, the blueish grey binding, the bluish night through his cell window. Pavlo lay pressed against the wall, and both Inquisitors saw him lying there, what were their names: Kafka and Villyay de Leel Ahdam. The third story, last in the book, was only seven pages long. Pavlo searched for the final word, it read "enough". Did that give him strength? What could Pavlo do but read it; he was already so radically transformed that he had to continue reading, and this time he read without expectations.

The story was called "The Fillip", and Pavlo immediately learned what that was. It was a light strike on the nose, just a single flick, on the bridge of the nose, or from the side, against a nostril. Often also just a snap of the fingers from below against the tip of the nose. The person meting out this fillip was a guard, and its recipient a prisoner in a concentration camp of the twentieth century. Pavlo, like everyone in Uniterr, knew what a concentration camp was, just as he knew that there were none in Uniterr and never could be.

A kind of amalgam of penal colony and an inquisition dungeon, that is how one was supposed to imagine this site, and in such a place, among the daily routine of torture and murder, a fillip was a laughable trifle. Nothing to make a fuss about, just like—Pavlo thought about it for a while, but couldn't think of a comparison. So he flicked his own nose, just a little bit of pain, which ran down his face, a touch of numbness of the skin between mouth and brow.—Was that all?—Pavlo flicked his nose again. This time it barely hurt at all. He flicked it a third and fourth time, faster, harder: not even a burning sensation: that's how quickly you got used to it. And this prisoner got one daily, during the morning roll call, a flick on the nose, not rough, just a flick on the nose, every morning at roll call, and it rarely even bled.—That is how things went for a year and nine months, every morning for six hundred and thirty eight days.—Six hundred and thirty eight flicks on the nose, thought Pavlo, and he flicked himself a fifth time: this time it stung; and that's when Pavlo suddenly understood that it might make a difference that it was the guard who flicked the prisoner. "So began the 639th morning."—The prisoner had no name, he was a number, 441 825, which he wore tattooed onto his wrist.—Pavlo, the book in both hands, looked at his own wrist: His number was not tattooed on his skin.—The author of the story was called "Anonymous".—"So began the 639th morning. 441 825 stood in the front row. He always stood in the front row on a direct order from the squad leader, the *Scharführer*, who stated that 441 825 must always stand in the front row. The *Scharführer* stood before him once again. He gave the prisoner a joyful look, as always. The prisoner, a fifty-nine year old man, stood at attention, as he had been ordered to do, the striped cap pulled off his head, hands pressed against his striped pants. "There he is, our little darling", said the *Scharführer*. "Surely he's been waiting for this all night." 441 825 was to answer "Yes sir!" while looking the *Scharführer* in the eyes. "Yes sir!" said 441 825, and his voice was dull and his eyes filled with terror. "Well then, good morning!" said the *Scharführer* and struck 441 825 on the nose, this time with a flat hand against the bridge of his nose. It was only a slap. 441 825 felt his face explode yet it was nothing, no blood was shed."

And on the next, the six hundred and fortieth day, again.—"441 825 stood in the front row as always, the striped cap pulled off his head, hands pressed against his striped pants. The *Scharführer* stood before him once again. He gave the prisoner a joyful look, as always. 441 825 began to tremble. ""There he is, our little darling", said the beaming *Scharführer*. "Surely he's been waiting for this all night."—"Yes sir!" said 441 825. His voice rattled; he closed his eyes. Deafening silence, no strike came. For an eternity 441 825 stood there, and for an eternity there was deafening silence, then 441 825 opened his eyes and saw the *Scharführer* standing before him. "Well then, good morning!" said the *Scharführer* and struck 441 825 on the nose, this time from the right, a little harder than usual, yet once again no blood was shed. 441 825 howled softly. "Well, well!" said the *Scharführer*. 441 825 stood silently. His entire head throbbed. The *Scharführer* laughed and moved on."—I'm going insane, Pavlo thought with his entire being.—"Every morning during morning roll call 441 825 received his fillip. Nothing worse happened to him. They went easy on him during labor, at the explicit command of the camp leader: He belonged to the potato peeling crew, and had nearly as much food as he could eat. He wasn't strapped to the rack for whipping, he wasn't thrown into the quarry, he wasn't hung from the limbs of a tree by his dislocated arms. He wasn't bathed in the toilet. Everyone in the camp knew him, and he was envied by all. Everyone wanted to know how 441 825 had obtained his privileges. 441 825 had his own bunk, though he slept no more than three hours a night, and even then he dreamed about the fillips and awoke screaming from sleep. His comrades would have gladly given him a beating, but that was strictly forbidden by the camp commander, and the block leader kept watch."—Now came the six hundred and fiftieth day. "So began the 650th day, 441 825 stood in the front row during morning roll call, and as he heard the *Scharführer* coming, he whimpered like a dog. He stood, as ordered, the striped cap pulled off his head, hands pressed against his striped pants, though he could not suppress the whimpering. Silent laughter sounded out from the block of prisoners. The *Scharführer* walked up to 441 825, who still could not stop whimpering. The *Scharführer* gave him a look of reproach. He's going to beat me to death, thought 441 825, and he saw it as his deliverance. The *Scharführer* looked at him in silence and then continued. 441 825 was still whimpering. He heard the *Scharführer* move on, and initially thought he must be going crazy. Then he thought that the *Scharführer* had grown tired of him, and then he thought that he had finally learned to do exactly what was expected of him. Nothing was explained in the camp. They would beat you for as long as it took to make you understand what you were supposed to do. One man was required, every day after noon soup, to stand on his head and crow, and he was beaten silently for as long as it took him to understand why. Now I get it, now it's over, thought 441 825. It was the happiest day of his life, yet he didn't sleep a wink that night. He thought that he was nothing but a dog, and he had to whimper like a dog, to whimper at morning roll call every morning of every day, until the end of his life, and then he would no longer receive fillips. On the next morning, the 651st day in 441 825's life in the camp, 441 825 stood in the front row as always, the striped cap pulled off his head, hands pressed against his striped pants, and the *Scharführer* approached. I need to whimper like a dog now, thought 441 825, and he whimpered. He was a dog. The *Scharführer* gave him a beaming look. "There he is, our little darling!" said the *Scharführer*. "He waited all night for this!"—The whimpering cracked into a stifled "Yes sir", a gasp, and a look, in which madness laughed. "Well then, good morning!" said the *Scharführer* and struck 441 825 on the nose. This time he hit the bridge of his nose again, and once again no blood was shed.

"I won't read any more!" cried Pavlo with his entire body.—Suddenly he understood the first story, and of course he kept reading, the six hundred and fifty second day.—"So began the 652nd day. Once again 441 825 had gotten no sleep during the night, he had wracked his brains for what it was they wanted from him: Should he whimper or not? He didn't know, and he didn't dare ask anyone. He knew that his comrades hated him, because he had received special treatment, since he hadn't been strapped to the rack or thrown into the quarry even once. During morning roll call, 441 825 stood in the front row again, the striped cap pulled off his head, hands pressed against his striped pants. The *Scharführer* approached. 441 825 was paralyzed by fear, his entire body trembled, he could no longer stand at attention, and he could no longer whimper. The *Scharführer* beamed. "There he is, our little darling!" he said. "Surely he waited all night for this?" From the throat of 441 825 rose a bellow of agony. The prisoners had heard every kind of scream a flogged man could make: howling, screeching, cries of despair, the cracking of whips, and the swinging of bodies from the limbs of trees, that was everyday life in the camp, but this bellowing made them shudder.

"Well then, good morning!" said the *Scharführer* and struck 441 825 on the nose. Once again he hit him from above, and once again no blood was shed. Shaking, 441 825 fell to the ground, foaming at the mouth. Had he been any other prisoner, the men standing next to him would have caught him, but they let him fall. He'd been given preferential treatment, they hated him. The *Scharführer* left him lying on the ground as well, and did not, as was his habit, kick the hell out of his kidneys. Then 441 825 went back to peeling potatoes. In the evening, in his block, 441 825 dared to ask his block leader what they wanted from him. He would do anything, but he was losing his mind. The block leader struck him on the nose, a flicking of the fingers against the tip, and sent him to bed. 441 825 whimpered throughout the night, curled into his horse hair blanket. He was one of the few to own a horse hair blanket. On this block, the only other man with a horse hair blanket was the block leader. For seven more days, 441 825 stood at morning roll call, the striped cap pulled off his head, hands pressed against his striped pants, and seven more times the *Scharführer* said: "There he is, our little darling!" and seven more times the *Scharführer* asked 441 825 whether he had waited all night for that moment, and by the third day, the prisoners had gotten used to his bellowing. That's how fast it went. Seven more times the *Scharführer* said: "Well then, good morning!" and seven more times he struck 441 825 on the nose, always from above, on the bridge of the nose, and not once during those seven times did he shed blood. By the six hundred and sixtieth day of life in the camp, 441 825 had gone insane. He could no longer peel potatoes, the peeler kept falling from his hands, he rolled himself into a ball, arms wrapped around his nose, and this time he was kicked, a kick in the kidneys, but even this kick could no longer drive out the madness. The *Scharführer* was notified. He came over with the camp leader and looked at 441 825 as he lay on the ground, arms wrapped around his nose, and he said: "Well then, camp leader!" and the camp leader repeated: "Well then!" and left. The *Scharführer* gave an order. 375 288 came running and struck 441 825 dead with a pickaxe. It only took one blow, that was enough."

And there it was: THE END, Pavlo read: "The End" and slowly, like a punch in the gut, a dull piercing of life and soul, Pavlo began to understand, and he said: "Our daily blow"—Suddenly he recalled a sentence from the end of the first story, which he had skimmed over carelessly, and which he knew he now needed to make sense of it all. He leafed back through the book, and as though each word had been waiting for him, the following jumped off the page: " . . . they were poor, oppressed people."

Pavlo clapped the book shut; the sky glowed violet outside the window to his cell, Uniterr sending its message into the cosmos.

"Give us this day our daily blow –"said Pavlo. He didn't know what he was saying, but he said it, just like that.

And then he drank.

THE END